THE AD MAN'S SUMMER

The Ad Man's Summer

Richard N. Anderson

Excerpts from *The Lost Chapters,* by Lisa Anderson reprinted with permission by the author.
Copyright 2013 © Lisa Anderson
ISBN 978-1-304-13045-7

Onion River Press
89 Church Street
Burlington, VT 05401
info@onionriverpress.com
www.onionriverpress.com

ISBN: 978-1-966607-03-8 paperback // 978-1-966607-04-5 eBook
Library of Congress Control Number: 2025912671

For Bruce

Ride my subway train from here to heaven
Ride my ferry boat up my muddy river
Walk our beach sand and our blades of beach grass
My New York City is the town, where I found you.

Woody Guthrie

1

Seventy-fifth Street between Madison and 5th Avenue in New York City looks like most Upper East Side streets in that part of Manhattan. There are rows of scrubbed brick townhouses with burglar warning signs on the windows and doors. Other townhouses bear the marks of dismemberment into apartments, two to the floor, with the characteristically messy-finger-marked brass mailboxes out front.

The tenant of Apartment 2-F of one of those sub-divided townhouses, 11 East 75th Street, was one of New York's most beautiful women. Beautiful, rich, and sought-after, she was New York's top fashion model.

She was five foot ten, half German, half Swedish, with hair the color and shine of caramel. She had the high cheekbones and the flat chest of an Eileen Ford model. Her gray-blue eyes brightened against a suntan from picture assignments in all the sun paradises of the world.

Her name was Lina von Stade. She was nineteen, a baroness by birth, and at six thirty in the evening on June 9th, 1967, she stood in the kitchen of her apartment arranging cold, raw fish on a plate next to a bottle of Polish vodka.

In the tiny living room the gray shag rug was splattered with the LP jackets of Gerry Mulligan and Gary McFarland records. A KLH Model 20 and a white telephone with thirty feet of wire perched side by side on a black wrought iron table under the bay window facing the street. A dusty palm tree in a huge wicker flowerpot-holder and a bleached, wooden high-back chair of Scandinavian design framed the table.

Lina came into the living room and put the tray of raw fish, two glasses, and the bottle of vodka on the floor near the table. She lifted a record from an album, slipped it over the spindle of the KLH, and snapped the auto switch. The record shivered down the shaft of the turntable, the tone arm snapped and fell slowly into position, and Gerry Mulligan and the Concert Jazz Band started to play "My Kinda Love."

At that moment, a tall man with a crew cut in a cotton seersucker suit with trousers slightly baggy from sitting at a big desk in a smart mid-town office turned west on 75th Street and walked into the late afternoon sunlight that shone across Central Park. He was on his way to Apartment 2-F, and he was smiling.

Twelve hours later he would leave Lina asleep, warm, and exhausted. Being careful not to wake her mother, who was sleeping on the Castro Convertible in the living room, he headed home ten blocks north on Park Avenue.

Alan Robinson didn't do this sort of thing all the time—only between Memorial Day and Labor Day. The rest of the year he was happily married and the proud father of two.

2

Alan must have set some kind of speed record for dressing and undressing on Tuesday morning. At seven thirty he stumbled into the john. He wasn't an early riser, and he'd returned to the city on a late train. He turned on WINS, "all news all the time" to hear the weather. The windows of his bedroom were so shrouded in soot and age that it was difficult to tell if the sun was out or if it was really morning. At least it wasn't raining; no gray drips ran along the forty-year-old window molding.

He looked around the bathroom to assess the cockroach population. Their numbers seemed to have been checked by the boric acid he had accidentally spilled on the floor the night before.

Halfway through his shave, WINS began its baseball score segment. He used to love baseball. He saw Don Larsen pitch a perfect game for the Yankees in the 1956 World Series. But so many new teams had spoiled the game for him. Or was it that the players were now younger than he was? The scores seemed relentless. My God, he asked himself in the mirror, how many teams are there in the majors?

A shower.

Light gray trousers and the stretch socks—most of the stretch gone out of them—and his brogues. A starched, button-down white shirt. He enjoyed ignoring the changing fashions. He made a point of dressing conservatively. The young guys told him he looked too square to work in the creative department, but he felt it gave him an edge with established agency clients and with his group. A red paisley tie and a light blazer and he was off to work, with a brief layover Midtown at the Berkshire Hotel, Room 215.

Lina was watching Hugh Downs on *The Today Show* when he buzzed. She had showered, splashed some totally unnoticeable fumes on herself that left a trace of fresh and sweet. She wore a soft white thing that went down to her knees with a slight collar. She answered the buzzer and Alan walked in.

"Lindsay is a Democrat," she said, nuzzling his neck with her face.

"Why should you care, you're from Helsinki."

"Yes, but he is your mayor and you should know these things." She had his tie loosened by the word mayor.

"If he looked like Abe Beame, he wouldn't be mayor of New York."

"Who is Abe Beame?"

"He's a little guy who always seems to be city comptroller but occasionally runs for mayor and loses."

Lina went to the TV set, turned Edward Newman down a little, and got into bed.

She watched Alan undress, carefully folding one part of his outfit after the other. He slid in next to Lina and kissed her on the side of the face. She turned, and side by side, close together, they just fitted; where she went out he went in and the other way around.

Then, just when Alan was about to make his move, riveters started their work on the new building going up next to the hotel, shattering the quiet.

Alan laughed. Lina laughed.

"That's going to be one hell of a sound effect for the next couple of minutes," he said.

"Minutes my ass," Lina murmured, biting his neck.

* * *

Later that morning a tall guy with long blond hair over his ears and a floppy mustache appeared in Alan's office doorway like he had something to say.

"Yeees?" Alan was on hold. He put down the phone receiver. Landon Weeks was the account executive on one of Alan's brands at the Dunaway Advertising Agency. Ten years younger, Landon was a real bachelor. His office was covered with hosiery ads, the models mostly nude from the waist up. Landon had the pixieish quality the girls seemed to go for.

"Boy, did I have a wild time last night, Alan."

"Oh? Step right in and give me the whole thing."

Landon plunked down on the black leather couch. "Remember the gal who used to work for Paul Curry?"

Alan didn't.

"The one who looked Irish but didn't dress that way?" Alan tried to remember.

"You asked me who she was, for Christ's sake. Remember?" Landon kept probing. "You said she dressed great but had a face like Floral Park."[1]

"Oh yes. Now I remember. She was kind of cute. She was the one who was always in those wool suits with lots of scarves." Alan admired the conservative Peck & Peck look.

"Well, she left the agency about a month ago. She went over to CBS. And then, she called me the other day and invited me to a party last night."

"Well?"

"What a chick, Alan. Remember, we were sure she was her clothes, well-dressed and petite and all?"

"You end up with her?"

"Yep."

"Any good?"

"Yep."

"On a ten-point scale?"

"Seven. Four. Seven."

"How come three numbers?" Alan asked.

"I rate on a three-count system, you know that."

(Alan didn't know that.)

"Sure. The first number is for movement and imagination. The second is for hygiene."

"Hygiene? Jesus!"

"And the third is for sense of humor."

"And what'd she get for hygiene? A four?"

"Alan. She is one dirty chick."

The two exploded with laughter. "Get out of here, man!" Alan chided, choking on his coffee.

"Alan?" His secretary Doris, a wise fifty-year-old from Canarsie in Brooklyn, stuck her head in the door. Her that's-enough-of-that face drove Landon to quickly wave and excuse himself.

"Lou has asked to see you at ten, I had the wine sent to Mr. Green like you asked, and Jo in research wants to know if she can meet with you tomorrow. Oh, and your dry cleaning is ready."

Alan enjoyed the way Doris spoke. She reminded him of his grandfather from Brooklyn who had said, "Cola Cola" instead of Coca-Cola.

"So, what's up with Lou? You always know everything before I do, Doris." Lou was Alan's boss, the creative director.

"Jane heard the word 'desperate' and something about the TransUS Airlines campaign."

"You're my favorite American spy. Thanks, Doris."

3

Alan couldn't take his eyes off the tall girl with close-cropped brown hair in a dirndl with silver buttons down the front, the Brother Rat's waitress uniform.[2]

"What's the matter, Alan? Haven't you ever dated a waitress before? That chick is sending you a lot of messages, my friend."

"Come on, Wally, Jesus."

Wally Hendricks sat with Alan at an outside table at Brother Rat's on 3rd Avenue. The outside tables were crowded today. The welcome cooler weather had drawn office workers out of the air conditioning.

The two co-workers had lunch together regularly. They had known each other since before Dunaway, and Alan found Wally entertaining. With offices on the same floor, in style and taste they were opposites. Wally spent a lot of evenings courting airline stewardesses. His hair was long. He took risks.

"Boy, I'll bet you get laid a lot." Wally picked up the menu.

Alan knew it by heart but pretended to search it anyway.

"Meatloaf bordelaise," Wally snickered. "Jesus."

"It's on the menu every day. Somebody at Warner Brothers must like it."

The tall waitress came over to their table. "Do you want to order, Mister Robinson?" she asked in a deep voice with a charming English accent.

Alan looked up from the menu.

"How'd you know my name?"

"One of the girls told me. She said I was waiting on Mister Robinson and Mister Hendricks."

"What's your name, m'dear?" asked Wally.

Alan cringed. Wally's overuse of that expression sounded more disparaging than affectionate.

"Else. E-L-S-E.

"What is it, German?" Wally asked as he ate the green celery top decoration in his Bloody Mary.

"Yes."

"Where are you from?" Alan had turned his chair halfway around so he could to look at her without the sun in his eyes.

"Dusseldorf."

Alan wished he'd been to Dusseldorf so he could say he'd been to Dusseldorf.

"Are you ready to order?" She smiled, slipping back into her Brother Rat's role.

"Cheeseburger, rare." Wally never seemed to order anything else.

"I'll have a double shrimp cocktail, Else." Alan handed the menu to her, and in a split second, she winked at him with both eyes, turned on a heel, and walked back inside the restaurant. Alan lifted his Bloody Mary and shook his head.

"God, she walks well, Wally. Did you notice?"

"Always a good sign, Alan. Might be some kind of an aristocrat underneath those Brother Rat's medieval wench threads."

"Maybe she's an actress or model or student or something."

"Well, I'll tell you something about Nick Ricci," Wally began, taking off his coat and draping it over the back of his chair. "He hires class. Gals on their way somewhere else who stop off in New York for a couple of months to make some dough."

"All thanks to the jet plane, Wally, and the low 'youth fares' these days. Oh, speaking of jet planes, Lou wants me to step in to oversee the Lucky Stores television work. Another trip to the coast, I guess."

They talked for a while, disagreeing about whether the amenities at the Beverly Hills hotels were worth the drive to the studios in Hollywood. Wally always stayed right in Hollywood.

Alan was thinking of Lina's fabulous eyes when Else reappeared with lunch. She put the wide plates down in front of Wally and Alan and, before they could register what was happening, perched on the two-foot-high flower box that screened the tables from the sidewalk. Leaning over, she took a sip out of Alan's Bloody Mary.

"I've never had one of those before."

Jesus, Alan thought. She took a drink out of my glass!

As suddenly as she sat and took the sip, she was on her feet and spinning away again, saying over her shoulder, "Don't want Nick to catch me with the customers."

"Christ, we're not customers," Wally yelled as she disappeared in the doorway. "We're fucking stockholders."

With a smirk, he turned his attention to his food, lifting the bun to shake salt on his burger. The cheerful voices of passersby rose above the noises of automobiles a few yards away.

"So, what's on your mind, pal?" Alan had finished the shrimp and was starting on his salad.

"I'm leaving."

"This sounds like something they say on daytime. Do you mean Dunaway?" Alan didn't feign surprise.

"That last round with the people from Cincinnati did me in."

"Yeah, that was ridiculous." An entire campaign scrapped because the client wanted to return to something more "traditional."

"So, I called Warren over at Baker and Dodge and they said sure, creative supervisor, and with a nice boost." Wally leaned back, waiting for Alan's reaction.

"No shit." Alan had expected an independent agency, one of the little shops. Now he was surprised.

"As far as I'm concerned, Howe can take a leak on his contract with General Soap. He screwed me."

Alan nodded. He didn't know the whole story, but he had his own sense. Agency President Bob Howe made deals. Wally was after splash, big concepts, abstractions. Another "artist" in advertising, he wasn't concrete enough to sell stuff. Howe, on the other hand, followed the client's intentions and had to close the deal. Alan wiped his mouth with his napkin and set it on the table.

"That's the business we're in, Wally. You know, Baker may not be any different."

Like a butterfly, the waitress Else appeared in what Wally called her "wench threads." She stood beside Alan, inspecting his plate, her blouse at eye level. He felt her hand lightly touch the back of his collar.

"Anything else, gentlemen?"

Alan and Wally looked at each other and smiled.

"Will you be here when we return tomorrow?" asked Wally.

"Maybe. Maybe not."

"Then my friend wants your number," Wally sneered.

"That's okay, Else. Just the check please."

4

Wednesday morning, two weeks later. Alan was stirring a small pot of Cream of Wheat on the stove. He had to have something to eat before he left today. He poured the gluey stuff in a bowl, added a little Vermont Maid syrup, and took a bite.

There are two kinds of summer bachelors. Those who live in their apartments and keep to the household routines, and those who let everything go. Alan Robinson was the latter. By the third year he had stopped keeping food in the refrigerator. When Liddie and the children left for the country in early June, Alan gave the cleaning woman everything that was still fresh or unopened. He hated the prospect of Liddie removing moldy leftovers from the fridge with smug derision at the end of August.

Most of the time it was too damn hot to eat. Some nights he went out with friends from work for a "liquid dinner." The typical summer bachelor lost about ten or fifteen pounds in three months. By September, people would come up to Alan or Tom Hartley or John Simmons and say, "My God you look fabulous. What are you on, the Canadian Air Force diet?"

Tom had the best answer at the Misquamicut Club when a local matron asked him the question. He looked at her, stuck a finger in his gin and tonic, and said, "I haven't had any food for three months." It was almost true. Alan and Tom used to joke that if the summer bachelor life went on without the weekend breaks with family, a guy would look like a prisoner of war.

Besides keeping food on hand, Alan's biggest domestic problem was managing the laundry. The basement of their building had laundry facilities (designed in the 1930s) but the Robinsons mostly went to a mom and pop laundry down the hill on 89th Street off Lexington. Like all laundries in New York, for a receipt, the Wong Family Laundry issued a slip torn off a larger slip with a date stamped on it. The idea was to keep the receipt, like a baggage claim check.

Inevitably, on an important Monday morning, Alan would find his shirt drawer empty. He'd rush to put on an old wrecked shirt, trousers, and loafers and walk down to the Wong's shop and hope that they were open—you never knew. He'd have to confess he had lost the slip and plead for his package of shirts. Usually Mrs. Wong was very nice, but occasionally the search for his shirts took about half an hour and, with other people coming and going, Alan felt worse and worse.

"What I need is a maid," he said out loud as he walked up the hill to the apartment this time. He got off the elevator, opened the apartment door, and dropped the bundle on the front hall table. He could breathe easy now. He had enough shirts for at least two weeks—unless a business trip sneaked up on him. He went into the kitchen and opened the refrigerator. A six-pack of Pabst, an unopened can of V8 juice, and a half a lemon were all the supplies in the Robinson household besides the Cream of Wheat, a half-filled envelope of crystallized iced tea mix, and a few cans of tomato paste in the cupboard.

The phone rang. It was probably Liddie.

He cleared his throat and prepared to sound like he was having a normal early morning, refreshed—but not the same refreshed that he felt after last night with Lina.

"Hello?"

"Alan, darling." It was Lina after all.

"Oh, hi."

"You forgot your wallet, your sunglasses, and your checkbook. Why don't you come over for them before you go to the office?"

He took the bundle of shirts into the bedroom. He was going to be late for work again.

Taking the subway after nine thirty in the morning, the crowds were always thinner. Alan stepped into the subway car and sat down for a change, his briefcase between his feet. He looked at his folded newspaper without taking in a word; his thoughts filled with work.

Alan needed a new writer. The TransUS Airlines account was manna from heaven. The question was, could Dunaway get the international routes? This was Alan's specialty, new messages for existing brands, but he and his group were spread thin. Since Wally left a week ago, the pace of things had exploded. Finding writers was hard under normal circumstances.

He'd have to start with the employment agencies who would sift through the resumes of people with bad reputations and frequent job changes to find that unlucky person lost in the pile with a solid resume and terrific talent. Times were uncertain in the advertising business. Rules of form and tone in sales messages had been replaced with fast and loose.

Wally kept telling him that evocative images told the story. Recently, what some clients wanted seemed to Alan to be racing toward the absurd. Trends were trends but Alan didn't buy most of it. So, maybe he'd find some guy thrown out for taking a risk or a guy who'd finally lost his cool. If nothing else, a screenwriter, someone fresh from the coast, or a humorist with some credits. He needed someone different. But by that Wednesday morning he hadn't had any luck.

He pushed the big metal doors to enter the enormous lobby of the office building. Ahead of him at the security desk the two building guards. They were both Black men; the heavyset one with hints of gray peaking from his cap chuckled at something the younger man had said. The lobby air was cooler than outside, but it would be thick and warm by noon.

Alan raised his hand to acknowledge the guards. Mr. Harris, the older man, returned the gesture. He had been at his station longer than Alan had been employed by Dunaway. An elevator car sat idle waiting for Alan to enter. He checked his watch and slipped in.

Avoiding the glances of the secretaries on his floor, he wove his way to his desk. Why was he self-conscious? They probably thought he'd been at a presentation or something, all of them except Doris, who knew almost everything. Almost.

* * *

Later, after lunch with Landon at the Bull and Bear, Alan strolled up 3rd Avenue for a few blocks. The stripes of sky between the buildings were murky gray, the air cool and welcoming. At the second corner he spotted a headhunter he'd worked with before his job at Dunaway. Alan turned and checked his reflection in the window of a stationery store. He hated these people. Their business was gossip. The light changed, and he crossed. He nodded a greeting to the lumpy-faced fellow with the shiny green suit on the opposite curb.

"Hello, Murray! Alan Robinson, J Dunaway Advertising." He put out his hand. "Glad I ran into you."

"I understand Gary Cross is in trouble at Pando-McCabe," Murray said, cocking his head to one side in a way that reminded Alan of an agitated reptile.

"Didn't know," Alan replied as they walked west on 52nd Street. "I know they lost some business, but they'd be nuts if they let Gary go."

"Well, they've got a new creative director."

"Oh?"

"Yes, Don McGrath. They got him from Levin and Moles."

Levin and Moles was supposed to be a "hot creative shop."

"I hear he's a prick." Alan stopped at the corner open-air fruit market and picked out an enormous red apple.

"Oh?" His companion looked at his watch, and Alan enjoyed a long moment. He knew that by disparaging a potential client, he'd violated the subtle etiquette.

"Incidentally, I'm looking for a writer. I know I'm supposed to go through the copy department manager, but since I've run into you, any ideas?"

"How much?"

That was always the first question.

"Oh, twenty. Twenty-two," Alan replied.

"Let me call you this afternoon."

"Okay. But do me a favor. Nobody with Volkswagen proofs, please.[3] Particularly Volkswagen trade ad proofs," Alan shouted over the traffic. He knew these days Volkswagen automobiles sold themselves.

Alan stood eating his apple slowly as the personnel guy walked away up Lexington Avenue. The kind of writer the guy's agency would send over would probably have proofs for products like Talon brand zippers, people who didn't know the first thing about selling seats on airlines, but he knew beating the bushes was the only way.

Back at the agency he got the number for the Holly Gelb Agency from Doris. Holly had a reputation for dismembering one agency's creative department and putting it piece by piece into another agency. Her company had flourished by selling the talents of young creatives who had won awards. It was like representing actors or actresses the day after they'd won the Oscars. The salary would skyrocket as agencies vied secretively for their competitor's new starlet, and Holly was on the receiving end of every negotiation.

Alan liked her. Unless it was about business, Holly didn't care what anyone thought. She was homely in appearance, but she dressed exquisitely. She had an incredible memory for salaries and who was working where.

Alan dialed.

"Holly Gelb, please hold on." The telephone operator-receptionist spat the words out as though she were working in the emergency ward at Bellevue. While he held on, Alan reached down into his refrigerator and took out a can of Coors Beer that he'd brought back from a trip to Denver.

"Holly Gelb Agency," the emergency room lady said again.

"Hi, this is Alan Robinson. Is Holly in?"

"One moment, please." The operator shunted him to an assistant, who also asked Alan to wait.

Alan took off the snap top of the Coors while he held the phone between his shoulder and his ear.

"Hi, Alan." Holly's deep voice and strong New York accent.

"How're you doing, Holly?"

"I just opened an office in London. That was them on the phone."

"That's terrific. Holly, I need a writer."

"You're not looking?"

"Nope. Things are fine. You want to have a drink later so I can tell you what I'm after? I hate to talk about matters on the phone, and I can't stand that cattle car office of yours."

Alan pictured the alcoves and booths at Holly's office where art directors and writers made out their employment applications. The most over-art-directed office in New York. People called it the Steve Frankfurt Memorial Personnel Agency (for the legendary former head of Y&R), a place Alan hoped to avoid.

"Sure, Alan, but do you mind if we go to the Stanhope?"

The Stanhope was all the way uptown on 5th at 81st Street across from the Metropolitan Museum of Art.

"Why the Stanhope? I thought I'd take you to the Sherry Netherland. You'd look so right there, Holly." He knew she went in for luxury, but she didn't pick up the tease.

"Well, I've got an appointment with my gynecologist at seven. And he's right next door to the Stanhope."

Alan chuckled to himself.

"Okay. The Stanhope at six."

5

Sunday night, Alan stood at the New London, Connecticut, station of the Penn Central Railroad waiting for the 6:33 train back to New York. He usually took a parlor car in the summer because he couldn't stand traveling with the Block Island crowd with their guitars and funny dogs and kids in slings.

Dave Chase walked up to Alan.

"Did you read the article about us in *New York Magazine?*" Dave spent his weekends on Fishers Island. Unlike Alan, he was shaved and dressed perfectly. Alan always got a kick out of the Fishers Island crowd. A lot of madras, straw hats, and mod watchbands.

"I can't stand *New York Magazine.*" Alan was cleaning his sunglasses with the tail of his shirt.

"Well, they have a piece about summer bachelors in it this week."

"What do they say?"

"They say we screw a lot."

"In what way?"

"Well, there's this one guy who leaves the Hamptons and gets off at some station and picks up some chick and they go someplace."

"You ever do that?"

"No."

"Neither have I. That whole magazine is bullshit. It's all about Fire Island and the West Side and how to do things cheap in New York. Just annoying."

"Well, anyway, you ought to take a look at this article. It may give you some ideas." Dave walked away.

"Hi, Alan." A tall blond woman in a pale-green silk dress approached him, offering her white-gloved hand. "Remember me? Polly Cartwright?"

"Sure. Polly, how are you?" Alan wasn't quite sure where he had met her, but the face was familiar.

"No. You don't." But her smile said that it was okay.

"My husband and I used to ride the grill car with you every Friday night."

"Oh yes." He did remember. The husband was an Englishman who worked in an ad agency.

"How is he?"

"I have no idea. We've been divorced for three years."

Here it comes, he thought. The long sad story.

"So, what are you doing?" he asked, trying to be earnest.

"I'm sort of a gal Friday to a couple of architects. Great fun."

"I always wanted to be an architect," Alan said. "I also wanted to be a lifeguard." And clearly you are confused and uncomfortable, he admonished himself.

"Do you take this train every Sunday night?" She asked after a sweet giggle.

"Yes. It's the last one before it's too late to get to the city. I'd rather arrive before eleven, even though there isn't too much to do back at the apartment."

The minute Alan said this, he realized that Polly had taken it completely differently.

"Are you allergic to cats?" She opened her purse and took out a lipstick, slowly sweeping it over her mouth.

"No."

"Well, I have three cats, and I'd love to have you over for a bite to eat later, if you'd like."

It's the old story, he thought. Look for it, nothing. Don't look, and it's "are you allergic to cats?"

"Gosh Polly, I don't think I can. I'm supposed to meet a couple of guys from Cincinnati who are flying in first thing," he lied. "But I'd really like to meet all the cats."

Polly flushed a tiny bit. Alan guessed it had been a fairly long shot.

"No, really." Alan was trying to restore the situation. "If it weren't for those bastards coming in for a copy meeting tomorrow, I'd be home taking an ice tray out of the fridge after we got in."

He paused and gave it his all. "It never fails. You see someone you haven't seen in a long time, someone as pretty as you, and you have to say 'I can't.' Very disappointing."

"Oh, I understand. I see it with my bosses all the time. Their poor lives aren't their own."

"Well, Polly Cartwright!" It was Dave Chase, madras and all. "Nice to see you," he said.

Alan walked away and over to a vendor who was also waiting for the train, his metal box overflowing at his feet.

"Do you have any gum?"

"Sure, eight cents."

"Thanks."

He looked at the gathering of people waiting for the 6:33 to New York and smiled. What a ritual. The minute they get settled, he thought, the Fishers Island guys will eat their watercress sandwiches and play backgammon. There will be at least one guy smoking a cigar, and I'll have to listen to the voices of a couple of business men from Providence talking about gold all the way to New York.

He felt badly about the Polly Cartwright invitation. Truth was, he would be at Lina's most evenings this week.

Jesus, he thought. Why does anyone do this?

* * *

After lunch the following Monday, Alan stood in the doorway of Tom Hartley's office. Tom was throwing small magnetic darts at a metal bullseye on his wall. Tom was a good-looking guy but only five foot six. He wore his hair longer than Alan's, and he rarely wore a tie.

"What a fucking business," Tom said without turning around. He had two of the magnetic darts in the second-best circle on the target.

"What's the matter?"

"Same old shit. Fucking client doesn't like the new radio stuff we did."

"I thought everybody liked it. Christ, I've gotten calls from friends of mine all over town who've heard it, and they think it's terrific."

"Well, they've got a new son-of-a-bitch over there who claims he knows a lot about music. He's close to the executive vice president, and he doesn't like the fucking music."

Alan knew he had to give Tom a few strokes before he asked his question. "You're good at this stuff, Tom, but we know how things work. See if Lou can figure out what's going on, maybe make the case with the numbers, but face it, you may have to start over. This wouldn't be the first time you have to kowtow to these idiots."

Tom rolled his eyes, but Alan had his attention.

"So, I need a favor."

"Of course," Tom said, throwing his last dart, scoring again. He turned to face Alan, gesturing for him to sit down. Tom knew when to return to business. He was a creative supervisor like Alan, a writer like him, and a loyal friend. "What can I do for you?" he asked.

"I need a writer for the TransUS Airlines account. Everyone is booked and Lou handed me some extra business with the go-ahead to bring somebody permanent on. Holly Gelb's looking for us—"

"That witch?"

Alan ignored the comment and continued.

"Before we hear from personnel, I thought I'd turn to you. Any names come to mind?"

"Not off the bat. But I can canvas later at PJs and see what I come up with."

"Someone with style. We need one of your young ivy friends. But someone who knows the meaning of work. No poets," Alan pleaded.

"No poets. No problem," Tom quipped.

"Don't jerk me around, I am getting desperate," Alan replied.

Tom smiled his wide toothy smile.

"I guess you just needed to think about someone else's problems to stop feeling sorry for yourself," Alan jested, pulling himself up from Tom's low, black leather couch.

"Funny, Alan." Tom sneered good-naturedly.

"By the way, will you be judging this year?" Alan asked.

"Nope, I wasn't asked. It was a load of work last year, but overall it was fun. Could be, as they say, that I can't recall the pain."

Alan looked at his watch. "Well, thanks for the help with the writer."

Tom was eying the dart board again. "You got it. See you later."

He headed for his office; calls to make and then some lunch.

* * *

Tuesday's afternoon group meeting was over, and Hugh, one of his copywriters, was telling a story. Their focus had strayed.

"So, anyway, Pete arrives at the gal's apartment to pick her up and go to dinner. She's all dressed and everything but she offers him a drink first."

"I'll bet they never go out for dinner, right?" leered Charlie Ogden, his favorite art director, who had joined them for some brainstorming. Alan leaned back in his chair, listening and observing the members of his group posed and perched around his office, standing by the window, half sitting on the fridge, leaning back in the black and chrome chairs.

"Right. But that's only part of it. Apparently, the guy this gal is married to is a little strange," continued Hugh.

"Oh?"

"Wait, wait! Where was the husband?" asked Charlie.

"He's away at a conference or something; Pete actually knows the guy. So, anyway, the way Pete tells it—and it is funny to hear him tell it by the way—they go into the bedroom, Pete gets undressed, then jumps in the bed and waits while the gal goes into the john."

"The way they always do," John added dryly.

"Anyway, in a minute or so she comes out wearing a two-piece, red, bikini-type thing. Sort of like a bathing suit, only made out of shiny silky material."

Hugh took a long pull on his cigarette. The others waited.

"So, Pete says, 'What's that?' And the gal says, 'Doesn't that make me look more sexy to you?' "

"What does Pete do?"

"He tells her to take the damn thing off. Then she goes into this thing about how her husband makes her wear this outfit before they go to bed to arouse him."

Both Alan and Charlie shook their heads.

"Well," John said. "I've read about guys like that. They need some sort of gimmick to get started."

"Okay!" Alan smiled but had had enough, and to make his point, rose from his desk. "Maybe we can continue this later," he said.

"If I were a gal, I'd tell the guy to fuck off," Charlie said as he got up.

"So! Back to what we were talking about before," inserted Alan, stepping into his supervisor role and attempting to be the adult in the room. "Charlie, can you take the 'castle with the moat' thing to the art department and get some boards worked up? That was a great idea.

"And John, man I know you hate to hear it, but we need an answer from research before we put everything into the 'turns on a dime' idea. I like it, but I want to go in solid to a meeting with those insecure bastards from Moline. No surprises.

"And everybody, remember I am in White Plains on Wednesday."

"I plan to be there, Alan," said Hugh.

"No shit. Let's go over the presentation tomorrow, and take your ashtray with you please."

Charlie Ogden made for the door, but the others took their time, putting their coke and beer bottles on the windowsill, picking up their pads, and joking about 'guys with problems.'

As they were crossing the threshold, John stopped suddenly—causing something that looked like a Marx Brothers pile up—to peer across the room past the secretaries' desks.

Charlie in his suede vest and sandals was there ahead of them, lingering in the waiting area on the way to the elevators.

"Well, hello," they heard him say with intention. "When you're done here, I need a girl Friday up one floor—and Saturday too, as a matter of fact."

"Move along, gentlemen." Doris, stout and unflappable, gestured for the copywriters to scram as she backed Alan into his office, out of earshot, and closed the door. The men from his group hung around in the hall, hoping to hear how the woman in the purple suit holding a black portfolio replied to Charlie's move.

"Alan, Miss Whitman is your three thirty."

"Sorry?"

"You are looking for a writer. For the TransUS Airlines account? Personnel sent up Miss Whitman's name on Friday after you left for the train. Here is her resume. Someone knew you were in a rush. I have two other resumes for you when you are done. Let's not keep her waiting." Alan had not expected the agency to help much. But Lou must have set things in motion, signaling to Alan not to waste any time.

Doris noticed the look of annoyance as Alan scanned the resume.

"Is there anything else?" she asked.

Alan groaned.

"A lady copywriter. They have to be kidding! I can't deal with female hormones and crap in my group right when we have two presentations and a new campaign," he said aloud.

But as he read, his expression became more puzzled. Doris noticed his eyebrows doing the dance they did when he was thinking.

"I thought you would prefer to meet her in your office. Shall I show her in?"

As if to himself, Alan read aloud: "Foxcroft... research at WOR, editorial assistant at Glamour." Impressive, he thought.

"Alan?"

"Yes. I mean, no. I'll meet her in the south conference room." He continued reading the resume.

"Certainly. Oh, and Alan? Liddie called. She found your sunglasses that you left in Pequot, and she wants you to call."

"Oh, brother. Okay then, give me five minutes."

* * *

Alan opened the conference room door and put out his hand, all business.

"Alan Robinson. Call me Alan."

Claire Whitman rose slowly reaching her hand to him. She was almost as tall as Alan. A long thin face, high cheekbones, and big wide green-blue eyes. She wore small gold, hoop earrings. Her hair was short and golden. Her grape-colored suit revealed a glimpse of a white blouse. Small top. Good hips. Great legs.

Her hand was cool, and she held Alan's hand firmly, elegantly.

"Please," he said, gesturing to the chair.

"Of course." A sweet fragrance like lilacs in the rain preceded her as she sat.

"Thank you for this interview," she said as he moved to his place at the other side of the table.

She arranged her portfolio so he could see it. She seemed calm, but she didn't look at him.

"Alan, I'd like to help your group as a copywriter," she began. "I brought some examples of my work."

"Of course," he said as he scanned the clippings trying to appear interested. A couple actually caught his eye, but he resisted the inclination to read them.

Instead he sat back and looked at the clock and then at Claire.

"So, personnel probably gave you the overview," he began. "We are looking for a full-time writer for six months with a good chance of becoming permanent. Someone with solid copy experience. Experience in..."—Here came the lie. He had thought this up when he was calling Liddie—"automotive and also commercial construction, particularly promotional advertising for floor covering trade shows. There are clients in these areas looking at our agency and, uh, so maybe you could point me to what you've got in those areas."

Whether because of her naive credulity or a determination to round any obstacle—Alan couldn't tell—Claire gave no hint of seeing through his attempt to disqualify her. She nodded, smiled briefly, and, completely ignoring Alan's speech, began to explain her portfolio of clippings. She landed neatly on her aspiration to be a writer, and transitioned to describing her current job at *Glamour*.

Alan didn't want to admit he was impressed by her. But he was; he actually listened as she spoke. For a moment he almost lost track of insisting on his requirements.

He watched her hands. He couldn't place her accent, northern but not New England. Private school.

"I get tired of explaining what I do all the time," she said conversationally. "Working as an editorial assistant in the lifestyle department."

"I know what you mean. Those cocktail parties where people come up and ask, 'what do you do?' and like an idiot I say, 'I'm in the agency business,' and from then on it's the usual, 'Oh, did you do the Alka Seltzer ads?'" [4]

"You mean you didn't do the Alka Seltzer ads?" She smiled her gorgeous smile at him. They had a repartee going. He was enjoying this.

"Well, that's when you make up something," she continued. "You're an undertaker or a labor organizer. That'll get them to leave you alone."

Her green-blue eyes flashed when she was making a point. He laughed.

Alan realized he had to wrap it up. She was talented, and obviously had some nerve, but nothing she could say could convince him to hire her to join his group.

"So, Claire. Why would a chick like you want to work for a group who doesn't make Alka Seltzer commercials?"

A pause. For less than a second, but for Alan an awkward eternity, the room was still. The curve of her smile straightened, and a look of composed disappointment landed on her face.

"Alan, you stand between me and my future. I am a college-educated woman with three years of relevant experience. Chicks go 'peep peep.'" She leaned toward him as if she was letting him in on a fact of life. Not a drop of humor in her mentoring, but friendly never-the-less. "I am not a chick. But I am interested in a job with J Dunaway Advertising."

Alan was nonplussed, embarrassed by his lapse. In courting Liddie, hell, in doing everything he had to do to get his own job, he had studied other people, manners, decorum, and all its intricacies. This was a job interview, you ass! But it crossed his mind that her response was exactly what would ensure she didn't get an offer from an agency. Well, certainly not his agency.

Claire's eyebrows arched expectantly, but without malice.

"You know," he began. "You caught me at the beginning of a brutal week, and I apologize. It has been extraordinary meeting you, Claire. We have a few more interviews to do, but I will have a chat with my managing director about your credentials."

He stood and glanced at the clock. "I have to head out of here as well. May I make up for my blunder by walking you out?"

She seemed to think for a moment, but replied, "Yes, that would be very nice of you. Shall I wait by the elevator?"

"Sure. Give me a minute."

6

"Hey, would you be chairman of the television part of the Gold Letter Awards this year?" It was Alan's oldest friend in the business, Bill Taylor. Alan and Bill had been copywriters together at Compton years ago.

Had it been anyone else, Alan wouldn't have answered the phone. He didn't believe in the whole awards business. Every year for five years the list of awardees read like a who's who of big client—big money—campaigns, no smaller shops. But when he heard Bill had been elected President last fall, Alan gave the whole thing a second look. If anyone appreciated good advertising, whatever the medium, it was Bill. He worked at a hit creative shop, but he didn't go in for fads or promoting people who didn't deserve it.

Barely a week since the announcement, and Bill was on the line.

"Jesus, man. Do I have to?" He half-whined, feigning resistance. He had a momentary panic. It would mean a bunch of evenings and probably was more complicated than he thought. What had Tom Hartley said?

As Bill began begging, an idea came to Alan. If I'm chairman of the committee, he thought to himself, I'll know everybody doing anything in TV. That's worth something.

"Sure, Bill. You got me. What do I have to do?"

"Well, you look at reels starting next Monday night at Ham Craig's Editorial Service on the Westside."

"How many reels?" Alan started jotting down the information. Lina was out of town. He had the time.

"Twenty."

"Twenty? How many minutes each?"

"Thirty."

"Jesus Christ, I'll go blind."

"Well, you got all week."

"You mean every night I have to look at a couple of hours of commercials. For a week?"

"That's it, man."

"Why so many, for God's sake?"

"Well, you know the old story. Levin and Moles submit fifty or so spots for the car accounts and another forty or so for the camera accounts, and..."

"You're kidding."

"Nope. And each submission costs twenty-five dollars!"

"That's unbelievable."

"That's show biz, my friend."

Alan shook his head and stared out the window at the fifty-story glass tower that interrupted his view of the East River in the distance.

"That's just unbelievable."

"I'm trying to get the rules changed for next year. But you will do it, won't you?"

"Well, it's a good thing it's summer. Sure. But don't I need a committee?"

Bill explained to Alan about picking his own committee.

"You can spell each other. Rules say you have to have at least three people looking."

Three people out of hundreds and hundreds of writers and art directors in New York City selecting what they think is the best advertising in the country.

Extraordinary, Alan thought.

"Well, I'll tell you one thing, Bill, it's going to be one helluva catholic committee. It's not going to be one of those Holly Gelb choirs. I'm going to get people from shops like Thompson and Bates and Pando-McCabe, as well as the big agencies who always get awards."

"That's up to you, man. In fact, I'm glad you're thinking that way because that's what I want. We need representation from everybody. The big agencies too. I have a couple of people in mind if you run out of names. Call me if you need extra people."

Alan began making a list of people he knew who would be good at judging TV ads. Long-haired Landon Weeks from accounts at Dunaway would surely do it. A gal who worked on the Procter business at Compton. A guy who had his own shop. A trombone player he knew who was an associate creative director at one of the big creative think tanks. For some reason, he began to write the name Claire Whitman, but stopped himself.

The list grew to twelve.

Alan buzzed Doris and asked her to come in.

"Doris, would you call these people in this order? Call them, and if you get them, buzz me. If you don't, leave a message to have them call me this afternoon. It's about the Gold Letter Awards."

Alan bet himself that it wouldn't take them long to return his call.

* * *

"Hi Alan. It's Laura Goldman." Laura worked at Levin and Moles.

"Want to serve on the television committee of the Gold Letter Awards?"

"Oh yes," she cooed.

"It's the sixty-second portion."

"Neat."

"There's a slight hitch, though, Laura. It's a week of looking. A whole week. After hours. Twenty reels. Thirty minutes each."

"Super."

Alan went slightly limp in his chair. Neat. Super. Right, man!

"Okay, I'll drop you a note with the time and place and anything else you ought to know. And by the way, keep this to yourself. They like the committee to be anonymous, at least for a while."

"Okay, Alan. And thanks, really. Thanks a lot."

Ten minutes later Doris had Chip Lucas on the phone.

"Chip, this is Alan Robinson. How would you like to serve on the Gold Letter Awards committee for television this year?"

"You want me?" There was a distinct sound of surprise.

"Absolutely. This year the Awards belong to the masses."

"I'll be damned."

"I would be very proud to have a guy on my committee who has personally supervised the largest automobile account in the United States. But frankly, I'm pretty sure none of your stuff will be in contention."

"Of course. It never is. They butcher the shit out of our stuff in Detroit. Just shots of wheels and deserts and girls on hoods."

"Someday I'd like to see what you really bring out there."

"It would kill you, Alan. It really would."

"Okay, I'll have Doris give you all the details in a letter. Appreciate your help."

The rest of the afternoon was pretty much the same. The previous Gold Letter acquirers blissfully accepted. The people who'd worked at agencies that wouldn't even let their people enter the awards, or who worked for clients who would have nothing to do with them, were flattered, surprised, and anxious for revenge. The next day Alan called Bill Taylor.

"Bill, I have my committee. It's going to be a lot of fun to see what happens in that screening room."

"Great."

"What about voting procedure?"

"Entirely up to you. Just so long as the rest of your committee feels good about it."

"Fine. Thanks, buddy. Talk to you soon." Alan hung up. For the first time in a while, he felt inspired.

7

The metallic harmonics of the new Electrolux vacuum cleaner followed Claire Whitman around the corner and into the bathroom as she drove the nozzle across the bumpy white tiles. She shook her damp bangs to be able to see.

Tuesday night, back from the holiday weekend, meant she had to clean before her roommate, Annette, got home. The apartment was so small that it was impossible to try to clean with the other person in the way, and it was Claire's turn to clean.

Flakes and crumbs vacuumed off the bedroom floor—that jingle was a safety pin!—celebrated their own Fourth of July as they rushed through the machine's steel tube.

Drips of sweat ran down her forehead and between her breasts. I feel like a coal miner, she thought, as she dragged the vacuum cleaner through the doorways of the hot little apartment. You aren't supposed to stretch the woven hose, she told herself, but how else to get into the recesses behind the sink cabinet?

At least she *had* a decent, modern vacuum cleaner, something her girlfriends with apartments didn't all have. She was grateful and had done her best to convey her gratitude to her parents at Christmas time—and to overlook their obvious suggestion. What would their twenty-eight–year-old daughter, an editorial assistant living independently in New York City, want for Christmas? Gee, a pretty new suit perhaps?

"Something to make life a little easier," Daddy had said. "No sense waiting for a gift registry!"

She knew they were weary of making excuses to their friends for why she hadn't married yet. Early yesterday, on the deck of the Katonah Country club, she had overheard her godmother murmuring sympathetically about "your brave daughter" as she poured another bourbon from her plaid picnic basket.

Claire's choices did not come as a surprise to her parents. Daddy had helped her get her first job editing catalogues for the journal, *The Musical Quarterly* (a long-running scholarly journal for writings by musicians and about music). But of course, she knew they worried.

The arrival of the dear Electrolux vacuum cleaner six months ago had added to her resolve to look for a more interesting writing job, and one that made more money. Most of the time the machine sat peacefully on its end in the closet, disinterested, solid, resembling Flash Gordon's spaceship. Its presence was a reminder of her plan and of the depressing alternatives back in Katonah. And, unlike her roommate, Annette, it forgave her for the many late nights she spent typing at the kitchen table and reading trade papers at the New York Public Library for her job search.

Claire used her toe to toggle off the switch, and the machine's roar stopped. She took a jug of water from the fridge and lit one of Annette's cigarettes; she didn't normally smoke. In the hot apartment, she liked the feeling it gave her. A little reward for her efforts, it was her dessert. The seat of the red vinyl kitchen chair felt cool but sticky.

Pushing aside magazines and Monday's to-do list on the kitchen table, she reread the beginning of her weekly letter to her sister. Betsy, who Claire called Suz, a mangled endearment for 'Sis,' lived outside Philadelphia with her husband Clyde, two children, and a golden retriever.

Dear Suz,

Much better week this week than last. For one thing there was a breeze. If only this apartment were on the street! It is tough to come back after the weekend. No joke.

Parents were on their best this weekend. Only one pep talk from Daddy on Sunday morning after he read the business section. Mom's thrilled that you and Clyde are coming up for Labor Day. Good decision.

I had two interviews last week. The one was interesting—writing reviews on a deadline, some corporate promotion—not my bag. The other was buried in a research department... but you never know, it's about getting in.

Claire reached for her pen and continued.

I really wanted the copywriting job at Dunaway Advertising, the big agency I told you about where I interviewed two weeks ago. I probably blew it (haven't heard from them). Just couldn't keep my mouth shut.

That exec was pretty typical. Not a business school type. He had radio experience in college, like me. I told him about Jazz Hour at Hollins. I was the first woman he'd ever met who'd heard of Django Reinhardt. Thought that would get me some points. Ha!

The rep at Gelb had said the job was for a travel writer, but the exec said they wanted construction equipment sales (??). I don't know. I like it at Glamour in some ways, but the department is tiny and everyone is insecure.

Oh yeah, last week I had two modeling sittings too. One was for the Lord and Taylor winter fashion catalogue—at the Pierre Hotel bar. Such a gas. So swank!

The big news? Cousin Chad wrote from LA and said he made art director at Decca (Records). Pretty neat, don't you think? He's begging me to come out. Says there are jobs galore. I love Chad. I may go on a scouting mission in August. (He said he'd pay!)

So, love to Marcie and Adam. Let's talk soon (on your bill).

Xo

Clairey

8

It had rained all day in the city on this Thursday in mid-July. In the late afternoon when it finally cleared, the sun setting behind the towers of the West Side apartment buildings across the park dripped gold. In places the pavement was still blue-gray with moisture. Alan and Lina walked slowly toward Lina's apartment. She was looking for her keys, digging her left arm into the immense bags that models carry—bags with appointment books bulging with numbers, reminders, and business cards.

He felt their manner was different than it had been when they first met at the Drake Hotel in May. Now it was mid-July. One of them would have to say it. Would he be able to? Alan realized the beautiful baroness was merely a girl in the sun, thrilled and awestruck by the big city, her new life, and the jazz-playing friend of a friend she'd met in a fancy hotel bar. She wasn't in love with him. For a moment in early June, those intoxicating first few weeks, he had almost lost his cool; weekends in the country with his wife and kids had been rough. He couldn't get enough of her. But, the lunacy of their pairing—the most beautiful fashion model in New York with a thirty-eight–year-old married copy writer—had begun to dawn on him.

Lina opened the door to the apartment.

"There is a party tonight, darling." She called him darling all the time, never Alan or Al. "Will you escort me to it?" Her blended Swedish-German accent had a sweet, sing-song way.

"Where are we going?"

"Here." She handed him a small brown paper bag, the size used at Gristedes Market for a pound of tomatoes. On one side, in bold

36

printed lettering, it said, "Pow! If you ever wanted to blow up a paper bag, hit this with your fist and make a big noise, then come to my studio on Thursday, July 12, any time after nine PM. It's going to be that kind of night." It was signed Lazlo Gerbelli, the famous fashion photographer.

Why would I give this up? He thought to himself. You know why, he answered.

"Make yourself a drink and then we can get some dinner." She puckered her delicious lips and kissed him. "I am going to freshen up."

He found the vodka where she kept it in the fridge and, creature of habit, poured a shot over ice in a glass. In the living room he sat and flipped through a copy of *Vogue*, appreciating the photography. Many agency art directors got their best visual ideas from magazine publisher Conde Nast.

He put the magazine back in the rattan rack and got up. He crossed to Lina's desk in front of the window. Her address book was opened to the page with his name. He smiled. She had beautiful handwriting. He noticed a pile of modeling vouchers thicker than a deck of cards. The one on top was for $1500. He couldn't help picking them up. $2000, $1750, $1500. She hadn't put in for these yet. Lina had been in the U.S. for a year making enormous sums for Eileen Ford, the grand dame of fashion modeling, and, so it seemed, for herself too. She was everywhere. *Vogue, Harper's Bazaar, The New York Times Magazine*. She said the advertising jobs paid the best.

"Come in here," she called from the bathroom.

"Are you out of the tub yet?"

"No. I want you to do something for me."

"What?"

"Shave me."

Alan walked to the half-open doorway. He opened it slowly, not sure what he would see. Lina was in the tub. Tan and wet, her hair in a funny yellow plastic wrap. She smiled at him coyly.

"Come in. Come in."

Alan walked slowly toward the tub.

"I don't know how to do that. What if I hurt you?"

"Don't be silly, darling. Just shave me like I was your face."

Shaving a beautiful model's under arms. This only happens in the movies, he thought.

"Do you use Gillette?" She said it like she was asking if he wanted cream and sugar.

"I buy anything that's in the sixty-nine cents store," he joked nervously.

She handed him a long, sculptured injector razor with sequins on it. The heat in the bathroom was uncomfortable. *The Burma Surgeon,* he thought.

"Okay, turn a little this way."

He ran his fingers over the soft skin of her armpit. Her seductive eyes didn't leave his face.

"God, Lina you do not need a shave."

"Yes I do, darling. It shows in the camera."

* * *

Later that evening Alan and Lina stood on the corner of 5th and 74th Street waiting for a cab. The muggy air created a dull yellow glow in the night sky above them. The streetlights hung as if in a misty scene from a film noir movie. Cars rushed past. Lina looked at him through blue-tinted glasses.

"Are you all right, darling?"

Alan nodded, then turned and raised his hand to hail a yellow cab, which of course flew past them. He felt awful but relieved. In her apartment, after sex, as they dressed to go out, Lina had told him she would be traveling in August and, knowing that the summer would have to come to an end, this nineteen-year-old had said what he had been thinking for a week now. Her matter-of-factness stunned him. No impressionable girl in evidence. She wasn't in love with him as he had imagined. Or if she were, she was a hell of a liar. A sweet liar.

"Do you have the party invitation?"

He pulled it halfway out of his breast pocket.

"Perfect!"

She put her arm around his neck and kissed his nose. He had become used to her affectionate gestures in public. She could do anything in public. She was that beautiful.

A cab pulled up, and Lina sashayed out into the street. She's hopeless, he thought. They got in, and she read off Gerbelli's address in that wonderful Swedish-sounding English. They were headed to lower Park Avenue. The famous photographer had a penthouse studio in the wholesale furniture part of the city.

The cab stopped at a half-lit commercial building on 28th and Park. The only light shone from the narrow doorway of the next building. Alan paid the cabby and got out. He ached, watching Lina walk away from him with her exaggerated fashion-model swing.

How can I give this up? He asked himself.

He sighed and followed her into the building. She took his hand in the coldly fluorescent lobby. A huge-eyed, tawny-haired girl, obviously one of Eileen's, was collecting the invitations—the printed grocery bags.

"Hi, Lina," the girl chirped.

"Hellooo," Lina replied, acknowledging the young model the way a seasoned actress would address an apprentice: she had no idea who the girl was. Alan looked at the floor. Here I am again with the star of the show. Suddenly he felt the familiar unpleasant awkwardness he had felt when he had first escorted Lina to functions: why is she with me?

He knew the feeling all too well. He had it at work sometimes. Like he was pretending to be someone. Like he was an imposter.

Lina led Alan to the freight elevator. The door opened very wide; it normally carried heavy equipment, backdrops, furniture, and lights for the commercial photography studio. It crawled upwards, dim brown bricks passing row by row, but he didn't mind. Lina pressed herself against him. She tucked her face under his chin and kissed him there.

He gently pushed her away and took hold of her face with the palms of his hands. His middle fingers were at her temples. He stared at her and felt a pain in his chest.

Suddenly the elevator door rolled open. A dimly lit room opened onto a terrace looking east with a low moon coming over the East River. A jazz band played. Voices greeted them. Greeted her.

Lina tried to introduce him but, in a moment, two skinny men with long hair and a woman with eyes made up like Eartha Kit had carried her away to meet someone named Franco.

Alan got a drink at the bar and watched the scene. The band played an arrangement of a popular rock tune that he didn't like. He leaned against a wall. Shrieks of laughter. Everyone around him seemed half his age.

I can't do this, he thought grimly. He took a swallow of gin, put his glass down, and walked to the elevator.

9

It took two weeks to select the winners. Finally, it was over. The fridge at Ham Craig's Editorial Service was left packed with extra beer and Coca-Cola from the committee's late nights in the six-story building on East 51st Street.

For years it had seemed to Alan like the awards had been either rigged or played awfully close by a handful of writers and art directors. Indeed, as Alan learned, the submissions were stacked. Anyone with a head for probabilities could guess at the results.

"So, how did it go?" Tom Hartley, the other Dunaway creative chief, was all ears.

"Well, the committee took matters into their own hands. Like a jury sequestered. One guy, whose wife is actually in admissions at Spence School, gave us a ranking strategy." They both laughed at that one.

"And to deal with the submission bias—that's what I learned to call it—we weighted the ads better if they came in from a shop with less than five other ads. Of course, crap is crap. It didn't take too long to get it down to a couple dozen hot contenders."

"You sound pleased," said Tom.

"I feel like I did something good for a change."

"Any regrets?"

"Ask me after the weekend. I forgot Liddie's mother's birthday."

"Well, tell her you are almost famous!"

"Exactly. Almost," confessed Alan. "It was one for the resume. Next year it will probably be the same shenanigans."

"Are you going to the event?"

"The ceremony?"

"Yeah, go and drink some of their booze. You deserve it."

* * *

Friday afternoon, waiting for the 5:35 PM Metro North train. Thick ninety-year-old air hung over the dispirited crowds in the Grand Central Station concourse. Through the haze, Claire could hardly make out the constellations painted on the gray-green ceiling far overhead.

A crush of travelers stood around, the usual Friday rush hour. Heat-related power outages and the national shopcraft unions strike had conspired to scramble trains all over the country. She watched the information on the huge arrivals and departures board change. As if to a magnet, suddenly people began to move across the enormous room to their gate.

The regulars were at the gates below ground already. Claire had been down outside Track 8 until she learned that her train was two and a half hours delayed, at least.

Uncertain of what to do next, she walked to the bank of phone booths on the main concourse level, around the corner from the 42nd Street stairs. Two other people stood waiting. She dropped her bag between her feet and reached in her handbag for her change purse just in case. Hopefully her parents would be home and accept the collect call.

A seersucker pant leg emerged from the last booth, followed by the rest of a rumpled businessman. No tie, white shirt sleeves rolled up, he picked up a brown leather briefcase and paused ten feet away, looking from right to left and then at his watch.

"Excuse me? Mr. Robinson, isn't it?" Claire recognized the J. Dunaway Advertising executive instantly. He seemed thinner than she remembered, handsomer too.

"Oh, hello. Miss Whitman, right?" Alan said, walking over.

"Yes," she replied as warmly as she could, adding, "Claire. From the interview."

She assumed J. Dunaway Advertising had hired for the position already. In the meantime she had interviewed with two other companies.

"Of course! It's nice to run into you." He said, smiling wearily.

"You look like one of those guys in the rent-a-car commercials," she ventured with a smile, aware of her own wrinkled, sleeveless navy dress.

"I am," he said with a slightly fake wilt of his shoulder. "I've been in Pittsburgh, and the traffic from the airport into the city this afternoon was unbelievable. I thought I'd try to make it to the country tonight, but it seems pretty unlikely."

"Yes. It's a lousy day to take the train. The board says two and a half hours for the train north, but I don't know whether I should believe it."

"Headed out of town for the weekend?" he asked.

"My parents have a place in Katonah."

"Well, the New Haven train is cancelled. I just spoke to my wife. There isn't another till 8:45." He looked at his watch. Claire noticed the veins in his tan, masculine forearm.

"Hey, what about getting a drink and a burger somewhere?" he offered.

"I would like that."

"Good. No use sitting around here. I already had my hot dog for the day."

"Oh look, a booth is free," Claire observed. "Would you mind watching my bag a minute? I need to let my parents know that the trains are late."

A line had gathered behind them. Alan stepped protectively toward Claire's leather-bound valise. CRW. He noticed the neat gold letters. I wonder what the R stands for?

In his mind he sketched a picture of Kornberg's on 43rd Street. The bar on the right. The menu on the wall. Was it too old school? Would they have air conditioning?

Claire edged toward the narrow phone booth, sat down, and pulled at the levered door. I can't believe my luck, she thought, smiling as she fumbled to find a dime to call the operator.

* * *

"I know a spot on 41st and Lexington, part bar, part deli. I think they have air conditioning. Want to try it?" Alan ventured.

"Sounds great, thanks. I have a couple of hours."

Alan held the heavy door so Claire could pass through. The air outside was stifling.

"Here, let me." Alan reached for Claire's bag. She couldn't quite hear him over the street noise, but she understood the gesture and passed it to him with an appreciative smile.

They turned and made their way slowly against the crush of grim, determined commuters headed into the Grand Central Terminal. The afternoon sun baked the pavement. In survival mode, Alan led them forward, attempting to stay in the intermittent shade.

He was pretty sure the place he'd chosen would still be there, although with urban renewal and changes in mid-town one never knew. Kornberg's was an old New York restaurant, not one of those fake places with English pub names. They inched past a newspaper kiosk and through a stream of people—older women clutching plastic shopping bags, young women with white wicker purses, businessmen in light gray and tan suits, laborers with lunch boxes. Alan turned to catch Claire's eye, offering encouragement.

Kornberg's was open. The maître d'—no doubt the owner—showed them to a table beyond the curved bar in the cool darkness at the back of the restaurant. Alan noted the checked tablecloths and red vase candleholders, the kind with netting on the outside. Nothing special, the kind of place his father loved, but this wasn't a date.

"Coffee?" A waitress in a black shiny uniform arrived with paper menus. The gold bubbles of a decorative neon beer sign illuminated her white apron.

"Is it too early for a drink?" Alan asked.

"Not at all. What would you like?"

"Miss Whitman? Claire. Would you like something?"

"A glass of white wine, please. And some water too."

"And for you, sir?"

"I'll have a very dry gin martini with some lime."

The waitress turned away.

"Well, what a nice treat," Alan began. "But that was something else. I don't usually find myself going upstream at five on Friday." He decided to relax, not to bother with formality. He rolled his loosened shirtsleeves, one and then the other.

"Scenes like that make you wonder who runs this city on the weekends. That was something out of *Exodus*," Claire said, moving her handbag and settling in to the booth.

"Do you go out to your parents regularly?"

"Every few weeks. I find plenty to do here, and I have some friends who have a beach house on the Jersey Shore. The city is still new to me, even after four years." She paused as their water glasses arrived. She had to take a drink.

"You must have a country house," she ventured.

"Yes, I'm a summer bachelor. While my family stays cool in the country all summer, I only get to escape on weekends."

"Oh, yes. That must be tough." Claire looked at him momentarily and then turned to the menu. She had met more than a few married men temporarily living the single life.

"What's the coldest thing they serve?" she asked, as if to herself.

Alan had immediately felt self-conscious repeating his usual lines. His cool delivery felt misplaced. Unlike when he sat across from the girl in the pale-blue Pan Am uniform at Wally's last week or at the Drake with Brad when he met Lina in May, looking across at this woman, words usually delivered with a certain meaning failed him.

They ordered food. Once the waitress brought their drinks, the conversation turned to college and early experiences in the city. When Claire described a piece that she had written for a lifestyle magazine about the airlines, the conversation turned to advertising. Alan told her about his experience creating print campaigns featured in magazines like *Holiday* and *The Saturday Evening Post*.

After a while, the waiter arrived with their meals. Alan picked up his gray-green dill pickle and took a bite.

"I think the lifestyle magazines will have to differentiate themselves eventually," she said boldly, as she added pepper to her salad. She felt the effect of wine and took a sip of water.

"How do you mean?" he asked.

"I think beauty is more than beauty, like travel is more than travel. There is travel to cities, the countryside, there is mature beauty and those who are interested in more than skin and hair."

"You speak in riddles."

She took a sip of her drink and said, "I think the magazines will eventually need to change their tone, and I think advertisers are missing critical markets."

As an observer of the advertising business, Alan thought Claire made good points. He had heard it repeatedly from his committee during the awards discussions. "This one appeals to the new ambition," one guy had commented about an ad. "It reflects the changing support for co-education," the gal from Compton had insisted. Alan had finally come around to the notion that an "idea" could sell sneakers, or luggage for that matter.

She reminded him in some ways of Liddie before they were married, or maybe of the woman he had thought Liddie was. He liked listening to Claire. He liked debating with her. He calculated their age difference.

"Independent women are spending real money, and no one is paying attention! I think the designers, publishers, and advertisers who really listen to them, to working women, will leave the rest standing there wondering, 'what happened?'" she declared.

"So, what do 'working women,' gals like you for example, what do you read?" Alan asked. He held up his rare roast beef sandwich, looking for an angle of attack.

"Well, *Glamour*, of course. *Cosmopolitan*, *Time*; I love *Art in America*. *The Atlantic*, the *Sunday Times*."

"Now you are trying to impress me."

"Well, sure." Claire smiled and speared a cucumber.

"I know a gal who is an assistant to the old lady editor at *Seventeen*. She says Sears should sell washing machines in fashion magazines. I've always thought she was nuts," remarked Alan.

"She's not. Get ready, Alan. One day there will be ads for Chevy trucks in *Good Housekeeping*."

"You are so wrong," Alan said smiling.

Claire took the last bite of her chicken salad. The man across from her seemed ten years younger than the advertising executive she remembered from that late afternoon in the beige offices of Dunaway. He hadn't mentioned their previous meeting, but she wasn't averse to bringing him up-to-date on her job prospects. Innocent of the eighty-year-old insider culture of big agencies, Claire was untarnished by impossibility. She felt she had nothing to lose.

"I kind of let you have it that day in my interview, Alan. Will you accept my apology? A job interview is probably the wrong time to reveal one's frustration."

"I thought I was being friendly. Complimentary, actually," he said, getting uncomfortable. Alan had been avoiding any mention of their interview. He hadn't asked her for an update. If he didn't think about it, he wouldn't have to consider that Claire may have been qualified for the job. And he had lied to put her off. He was doing all he could to suppress that thought.

Claire smiled. "Groupies at rock concerts are chicks, Alan. In an interview, would you like it if I called you a stud?"

"I certainly would!"

They both laughed, their discomfort relieved. Alan had scored a point and kept his cover. Claire had a good-natured way of showing her annoyance, he thought.

Claire let him have his moment. She tried to seem good-natured. He was nice. But like a lot of men, he took a lot for granted. A typical guy, but not a creep. He was handsome, but she was not interested in him romantically; she just found him interesting and funny. She looked at her watch.

Alan scanned the restaurant for their waiter.

"So, plans for the weekend?" Claire asked.

"Taking the boys to the beach, I hope, and eating a soggy grinder in the sun. My kind of heaven. How about you?"

"I'm looking forward to a paddle on the lake," she replied.

When the bill came, she attempted to pay her portion, but then easily gave in and let him take her out. They parted back at Grand Central Station as the huge black announcements board, clicking away, showed her track number. Just like that, they had become friends.

10

"Remember the newscaster I saw briefly? The gal with the Warrenton, Virginia equestrian look that you liked?" Tom Hartley leaned forward in one of Alan's designer chrome and vinyl director's chairs, sipping coffee from a glass mug.

They all know my style, Alan thought. "Yeah, I seem to recall something about you watching her show on TV while you ate dinner with your wife," he said.

"Well, she goes to a psychiatrist because she's got this thing about married guys."

"She can't get enough, right?" asked Alan.

"No, she's riddled with guilt!"

"Oh, come on," Alan sneered. "If that were the case, every dame in the city should be going to a shrink."

"What do you mean?"

"I've done my own research on this topic. While it may come as a surprise, every gal I've ever interviewed—" Alan paused and adjusted his tie for effect. "—would rather go out with a married guy than a single guy. No shit. And they prefer, thank God, an older married guy. Apparently, we're better."

"We are?" Tom looked skeptical.

"So, anyway, are you going to see her again? I mean in real life?"

"Bet your ass."

"What did you tell her about yourself?"

"Happily married, father of two. Greenwich. Harvard '52. The usual."

"That's what you said? Trying to put her off or trying to turn her on?"

"Yep."

"And she still…"

"Alan," Tom interrupted. "You want to know something? I don't think they give a shit. I don't think anybody gives a shit come to think of it."

"Well, that gets to our don't-give-a-shit theory. Remember that?"

"Funniest evening I ever spent."

"No, really. Nobody gives a shit. Remember, we had about five or six really-don't-give-a-shits. What were they? I know, the war in Indonesia was one."[5]

"And Raquel Welch. I mean, nobody gave a shit about her."

"Albert Shanker. Remember him? Nobody gave a shit about Albert Shanker."

"As I remember there was a little cruelty in the whole thing, though," Alan said. "It's easy not to give a shit. But all you have to do is talk to somebody whose house was washed away in the Agnes hurricane or Diane or one of those numbers—"

"Don't get sanctimonious on me, Robinson."

The gag had started the year before when they were both in Stockholm on business, tight and bored, waiting for a late overnight flight. The 'don't-give-a-shit' theory had arisen from Tom's rant about *The New York Times'* relentless coverage of certain world events. Taking a pencil from his briefcase, Tom had written notes for their own faux *Times* front page.

Alan chuckled remembering their fun. Nobody gave a shit because *The New York Times* was the same every day. And the *Sunday Magazine* was even worse. There was an article about the common market. One about the Democratic Party, one about Burt Bachrach, and some impossible recipe by Craig Claiborne. And, of course, one about a house built on Fire Island by a designer who found a new use for 'inner space.'

"We never get to the second page of the *Times!*" Tom lit a cigarette, snickering. He tried to suppress a coughing fit.

"Worse than the front page," Alan continued.

"Absolutely."

"All men's fashion ads, some article about Africa, and one of those George Lois Restaurant Associates spreads."

Alan looked at his watch.

"Are you going to PJ's later, Alan?" Tom sat up and tightened his tie. He always loosened it when he came into Alan's office.

"No, I've got a date. That gal who applied for the writer job that Buck Jones got." Alan tried to look nonchalant.

"Christ, you sure come up with the surprises."

"It turns out to be the only way." Alan skittered along in the river of bravado. He couldn't help himself. The frenzy and pleasure of the competition was heightened by the coffee. Tom looked at him expectantly, daring him, a half-smile, his eyes pulling Alan along.

"Any good?"

"Very pretty. Smart. Very big on the women's lib thing. I called her a chick and believe it or not, she said something to the effect that she wasn't a chick; she was a woman or a person or some bullshit. She actually said, 'chirp chirp!' "

"What? No wonder she didn't get the job."

"Later she said, 'would you like me to call you a stud?' And I said, 'I certainly would!' Interesting lady."

They both laughed, but in the pause that followed, Alan felt a little sick, like he missed his mark, went too far, an unsavory finish.

Tom finished his coffee. "Now I really forget why I stopped in."

"Maybe something to do with the Lucky Stores account?"

"Oh yeah, do you need anything for your trip to the coast? Sounds like things are pretty well set up, scripts are already out there. I was pulled in to work on things here, so I'll be curious how it goes."

"I'm sure it will be routine, although it is someone else's account. I haven't worked on grocery store chain advertising in years. Like the kids say now, it'll be a 'flashback.'"

* * *

The next week things came together for Alan. Finally, they had a new writer. Someone to help the agency get the international routes for the TransUS Airlines account. The young man from Colorado had joined Alan's group at the end of June.

"Buck Jones?" Everyone asked when introduced to him.

"Yep," Buck would answer.

Buck grew up in the city of Denver but had spent weekends with his family in a small, abandoned mining town. He told Alan that for kicks they would go out and shoot things with handguns—signs or beer cans, but occasionally a rabbit or a scruffy dog.

Buck went to college in the East. He had designed and written for his college yearbook, winning every award given to yearbooks, including one from *Life*. Somehow, he acquired knowledge of how the Easterner exhibited self-doubt and insecurity as skepticism. He could see into the collective psychology of gun-toting Westerners as well.

Buck had never written an ad or a commercial when he landed his first job at Thompson Bates, a rival agency. But in one year there he had half a dozen campaigns to his credit. In his interview he showed Alan a portfolio of commercials that he had written and produced, as well as pages of ads he'd written and art directed in *Life, Look,* and *Reader's Digest*. Buck had so impressed Alan that Alan hired him on the spot.

Buck walked into Alan's office mid-morning two weeks after he started his new job, smoking a handmade cigarette.

"Wanna have lunch today, Alan? We're going to make up the new account list for my agency."

"What are you talking about?" Alan looked confused.

"Didn't I tell you about my fake agency?"

Alan grinned. "Your fake agency?"

"Yeah," he said in Colorado twang. "I hate *Ad Age* so I started a fake agency."

John Simmons from TV production walked in while Buck was in the middle of his sentence. He sat down and looked at Alan, half quizzical, half smiling.

"I have no idea what you're talking about," he said.

Buck resumed.

"You see, I went to school with the grandson of the founder or the publisher or whatever of *Ad Age*. The kid was a pain in the ass. So, a few years ago I decided that I'd do a number on his old man's magazine."

Alan looked at John.

"Well, that's not quite accurate. What it was was, that I realized when I was in graduate school—"

"I forgot you went to business school!" Alan interrupted.

"Yep—I realized how inaccurate *Ad Age* was. And what a waste of time."

"So?" Alan said, pushing a small pile of work requests into a letter-box.

"Well, you know that issue they have every year telling what agency has what account and how much their billing is and who the people are and all that shit?"

"Yes."

"Well, that's when I decided to put *Ad Age* on."

"You created an agency?"

"Yep."

"What'd you call it?" John asked.

"Jones, Wiley, and Melcher."

"Who are Wiley and Melcher?" Alan wished he'd thought of the idea himself.

"Well, Willy Wiley is a media guy at Thompson Bates, and Charlie Melcher runs a gas station in Denver."

"Jesus, what an idea."

"Anyway, the first year we wrote to *Ad Age* for the forms to fill out about how big you are and your growth projections and all that crap. They sent them back, so we filled them out."

"How big were you when you started?" Alan asked as though everything were really true.

"We billed about seven hundred thousand."

"Where were your offices?" Simmons asked. John was very logical and orderly.

"My parents' house. 443 5th Avenue, Denver. That was our address."

"No shit."

"What accounts did you have?" Alan had swiveled his chair around, facing the young copywriter with the western boots and shaggy hair.

"We had Mom's Bread, Western Colorado Fencing Corporation, and the Sky-High Ski Trails account."

"That's fabulous." Alan and John were laughing so loudly Buck nudged the office door closed.

"Oh Jesus. You are something." Alan caught his breath. "So, where's lunch?"

"That place owned by the Chinese football player, or whatever he is, Dewey Wong's, over on 3rd and 58th."

Alan went there once a week. "I can't miss this. Okay if I join you?"

"Yep, see you at one." Buck turned in his cowboy boots and strode out.

11

"So that's it. No one's fault." Liddie tried to sound resolute as she rehearsed. She glanced in the rearview mirror to check traffic as she changed lanes before the downtown exit. No rush. She had at least half an hour till Alan's train arrived.

Rehearsing was so awkward, but it helped to fend off her heart-bumping terror about the conversation to come. Funny that she was finally using advice she had learned in junior college about public speaking to prepare to talk to her own husband!

Speaking aloud had calmed her for a few minutes, but now, her mind began to take off.

What will become of us? The children, all the furniture, dishes and the silver? she thought. Then, looking at herself again in the mirror, she panicked. My mascara! What if I cry? What was I thinking, getting all dolled up?

Friday nights Liddie always had her hair done and wore something flattering for Alan. But this evening? They had been invited to Thor and Emerald's for drinks, and since she had a sitter, of course, she accepted. Why not plan to go? Normal might be exactly what's needed tonight.

She had known this day would come ever since Easter. That Sunday in April something had begun to change, like stepping over a threshold. After church—Alan never went to church—before family Easter lunch with her parents, she had once again found herself making excuses for Alan at the annual Easter egg hunt holiday party for the Pequot Acres neighborhood association.

Alone, drink in hand, she had followed slowly behind her youngest son as he scampered from tree to tree, loading his basket with color. Across the garden other mothers had fused into a noisy menacing swarm of silk scarves and pillbox hats. Were they talking about her?

Ben Richardson, their neighbor in New York and an old high school summer flame, came along with his drink. His daughter was hunting for eggs too. They smiled their greeting and stood together, quietly watching the children.

Then something happened. Ben took a chance and asked the obvious question.

"Where is Alan?"

Maybe it was the way he asked it. Maybe it was his familiar gray eyes. At that moment he looked into her heart. Balancing in her powder-blue heels beneath the aromatic cedars, among the clumps of cheery daffodils, she had meant to say something practiced: "He had to take the early train," or "he had some work to finish." She was used to it.

Instead bitter tears welled up. She lost her balance and lurched toward a tree, and Ben had caught her.

"Ben, it is so hard!" she cried into his blazer.

A few weeks later they had run into each other at the market in New York and it had come out that he and Dee Dee were separated. He had been cautious about telling anyone, he said. Lowering their voices at the market by the potatoes and onions, she had felt like they were fellow agents sharing reconnaissance. They both knew divorce and separation were taboo. Shunning was not uncommon in Pequot and in the city as well.

It wasn't an affair at first. This summer, Ben had maintained his distance when he came to Pequot, although they both felt the old attraction and had said as much.

They had met twice privately, once by accident while walking at the beach, and one Saturday when Alan was sailing. They had discretely passed an hour in side-by-side lawn chairs while both of their kids were in lessons.

They shared the details of each other's marriages, talking like reunited castaways. Liddie devoured the recognition and understanding Ben offered her. His male perspective also helped her acknowledge the reality of Alan's total absorption in his work and the real reason for his frequent absences.

And then she had stopped by Ben's boat.

She knew he would be working on it at the marina on Tuesday during his vacation. So, on a gray afternoon two weeks ago, when the boys had an invitation to the movies, she went. She parked near the marina and walked over. She feigned a casual visit—"I was out shopping"—and held up some grapes in a brown paper bag as evidence.

Ben gave her a hand stepping on board, and that was it. A few minutes later they were in the bow having frantic sweaty sex. Had she planned the whole thing? Not exactly, but she knew that week that the timing would be pretty safe.

Afterward, they had laid back on the canvas bunk listening to the hollow patter of waves on the hull. Ben suggested a swim and then drove the boat out to the middle of the harbor so they could jump overboard. Later, back at the dock, they had eaten the grapes, apologizing and laughing. It wasn't going to lead to more, Liddie was certain. Ben was from her past. He understood.

That was weeks ago. They'd been fine since. Ben's strength had given her the resolve to face Alan tonight. She would name their dilemma.

"I am unhappy, and I don't think I love you anymore," she would say. Would he be shocked? Would he promise to take more vacation time off? Apologize for the latest working weekend? Tell her she was cruel to blame him for being stuck and bored in the hot city? Would he deny having another of his affairs? Would he accept her own as a desperate move in her own loneliness?

She knew what came next, and it wouldn't be easy.

Tonight, mascara would run and they might not make the party, but at least they would have a direction.

She parked the car out of the sun near the section of the platform where the wooden mail carts were parked. The train bell clanged as the huge, diesel engines lumbered around the corner, blocking the harbor view. The front few cars seemed to lean into the station, almost touching the roof. Station workers got busy, a conductor stepped down from the train, passengers gathered. Liddie got out and stood by the car. Alan knew where she'd be.

The train whistle blew, and there he was. But who was with him? Another man, his tie off, briefcase and leather bag in hand. He'd brought someone up for the weekend without telling her? Liddie squinted behind her dark glasses. Oh, it was only Peter Wells! Peter had a summer house in Pequot. She felt nauseous but relieved. She'd been wound so tight. Change of plans, she told herself, no big talk. But maybe that was okay. Had she just been saved? Maybe so. Just act normal. Breathe, she told herself.

"Hi Sweetheart. Okay if we give Peter a ride?"

"Hi! How was the train? Hi, Peter! Sure! Climb right in."

12

The studio offices of Parkwood Kahn were on West 45th Street in an old narrow commercial building with the world's slowest elevator. A Pinkerton guard sat beside a dead potted tree on a folding chair reading the *New York Post*. He looked up when Alan came in and jerked his head toward the elevator door. The guard had already shepherded a hundred people to the elevator. P-K was having a party, and he had to work a double.

Tonight was Alan's last night in the city before he flew to the coast. He had spent the weekend in the country making amends to Liddie in advance—taking the boys to their lessons and dressing up to take her to the inter-club dance—in case he would miss next Friday night. The children were adorable, but he felt like Liddie couldn't be bothered with him. He was her relief pitcher, nothing more.

Lou, the agency's creative director, had asked Alan and Tom Hartley to show up at the party so he could talk to them about the Lucky Stores account. Alan had taken over the account, and Tom would be his contact back in New York if he needed anything.

All the resemblance to the Parkwood Kahn lobby ended as soon as the elevator door opened on three. The studio reception area had a spaceship quality: stainless steel, black leather, and white plastic. He lingered a moment, collecting himself before entering the crowd. He didn't feel like getting into conversation yet.

Framed awards covered the walls. Most were for "excellence in film production," awarded to Mannie Kahn as cameraman and director from the Art Director's Club, the Copy Club, The Hollywood International TV Commercial Festival, and on and on. Alan had never heard of most of the groups.

The place was jammed. Voices ricocheted off every shiny surface, and there were a lot of them. The receptionist's desk had been transformed to a bar, complete with a bartender in silver waistcoat. Alan could see Mannie himself pouring drinks at a second bar down the hall in his office.

He knew or recognized most of the people standing around the reception area. As he made his way to order a drink, he nodded his acknowledgement to one or two.

"Hi A," Wally Hendricks, hair curled behind his ears, sporting a new mustache and granny glasses.

"Hey man! I almost didn't recognize you." They shook hands. "Does it help you write better?" Alan took in the wool-plaid-bellbottom slacks and velvet jacket with flared lapels, bright red and white striped shirt, and tie so wide the sides disappeared inside the jacket.

"No man, but the clients dig it."

"Things must be good at Baker," Alan said, but before Wally could answer, it was their turn to order drinks. The two made their way slowly down the hall through the smoke and the shouted conversations. Tom appeared through the mass of people carrying a glass safari style over his head. They found a corner to occupy while they watched for Lou.

"So, how are things with the baroness?" Wally asked.

Alan waved his hand as if refusing a refill. "No more models."

"Alan has a new interest," Tom leered. "You should have brought her."

"To this meat market? No, she's a serious writer. This wouldn't be her scene." Alan reached for fantail shrimp on a passing tray.

"What are you working on, Wally?"

"Baker stuff. Crowns cigarettes. Some food accounts."

"Hello Wally." Laura Goldman from the awards passed the men carrying a Bloody Mary and wearing a red satin dress. Wally turned to follow her.

"So?" Tom wanted the dirt.

"What, so? No comment on this one. Have you ever rented a convertible in Hollywood?" Alan changed the subject and, politely, Tom followed his cue.

"You'll sweat your ass off and you'll look like an out-of-towner. Nobody drives convertibles unless they're Italian convertibles. Where are you staying?"

"The Beverly Hills. Where I always stay." He took an eggroll offered by a redhead in hot pants.

"The terrace or the bungalows?"

"The terrace."

"The last time I stayed there all I got was a lousy dried-up basket of fruit."

"Yes, but as soon as you pick up the phone to make a call from your room, a delicious-sounding chick at the other end says, 'May I help you Mr. Robinson?' "

The banter continued.

Alan scanned the crowd for Lou. The room was hot, and he wanted to leave. What had Claire said when they walked off the Staten Island Ferry on their "date?" (What had possessed him to take her on the ferry a week ago?) "Can you imagine what it must have been like for someone to see the city for the first time?"

As they had watched from the upper deck, the trees at Battery Park had come into focus. The last sparks of sun had glinted on the windows of lower Manhattan. They had talked about Melville, Stéphane Grappelli, her first job at *The Musical Quarterly*, and martini olives. She took him by surprise in so many ways. Especially her job offer from Decca Records—she hadn't shared any details—and he hadn't asked. When they had parted at her building, she had placed a hand on his chest, said "this was really nice," and turned away.

The noise of the party brought Alan back. Tom had wandered away. Alan had to find Lou and then get out of here. As he turned, he recognized Kahn's secretary, whose arms were around an art director he knew. He worked his way further down the narrow hall toward Kahn's office. A hi-fi was playing Latin music somewhere. Tom stood near the bar with his back to Alan, already talking to Lou.

"There he is!" Lou exclaimed.

"Here I am," Alan replied.

13

Alan looked at the San Rafael Mountains from his first-class seat in the 707. His thoughts rambled on as the plane continued descending into what the stewardesses always called the "Los Angeles area." Airline language was a collection of redundancies.

He had come to California to shoot some Lucky Stores commercials with the comedian, Brook Henry. Everyone was talking about Henry. He'd made a splash on *Dick Cavett,*[6] *The Tonight Show,* and other late-night talk shows. Alan had never seen him. Who had the energy to stay up that late?

Lucky Stores was a big contract. It had taken a long time to negotiate. Then, when the creative supervisor on the business had had an appendicitis attack, Alan had volunteered to oversee production. It impressed the client that the creative department had assigned another copy chief to keep production moving. Alan liked the idea of a trip to the coast. It had been over a year since he was there last, and anyway, the thing with Lina was over. And Claire? That wasn't really a thing.

** * **

He checked into the Beverly Hills Hotel. Several messages were waiting for him at the front desk. The desk clerk slid the envelopes to him with one hand and gave the key to the bellhop with the other. Man, Alan thought, this guy must play poker.

The messages were the expected. His producer had arrived a few days earlier to look for locations to shoot. The commercials were supposed to take place in supermarkets, and both the agency and the client wanted the real thing, not a mock-up.

"Hi!" the second message read. "Welcome to Lotus Land. See you at eight for breakfast tomorrow morning."

Alan cringed at the reference, but to the locals he was just another hungry animal let out of his cage. Agency men, especially from the Midwest, transformed when they arrived in California. It was almost expected—bizarre clothes, smoking clove cigarettes, and worse.

The next morning Alan woke before his wake-up call. After dressing he had enough time to step outside. The pool looked serene through the huge windows, but the jets and pumps and fans thumped and whirred unpleasantly. He wove his way among the damp tables and lounge chairs. When the Mexican cat skimming leaves off the deep end noticed him, he nodded and quickly disappeared.

Newspaper under his arm, Alan entered the Lanai Room, with its green banana leaf wallpaper. He paused at the podium, taking in the muted elegance, inhaling the coffee, bacon, and cigar smoke. The same lady who'd been seating people at breakfast for the past two hundred years smiled like she was glad to see him. She led him to a table against the glass doors that separated the room from the patio outside.

"Hey, Alan!" He recognized the voice of the film studio's producer, Mel Fox. Mel was sitting in a corner banquet with three people Alan didn't recognize. They all wore those colorful Hollywood sweaters, cardigans with the slightly puffy sleeves in soft peach and lemon. He walked over.

"Alan, I'd like you to meet Hank Knox, the production manager; Lila, our makeup lady; and this is Brook Henry's agent, Corey Berger."

Alan shook hands. He knew he would promptly forget all these names.

"Have a good flight?" Mel asked.

"The usual. Mind if I pull up a chair?"

"Of course not, sit down." The waitress returned with a place setting and a pot of coffee.

"So, what's the story? What do we do today?"

"Well, we've found a couple of locations I think you should see, and then there's the casting session this afternoon."

"Do I have to go around looking at supermarkets, Mel? If *you* like it, and if it's technically okay, I'm satisfied."

Mel Fox was an Irishman, originally a New Yorker—a little slick but very funny. He was good at what he did; that was the important thing.

"Okay." Mel turned to Hank Knox, the production manager. "We'll skip the locations. Hank, why don't we try to move the casting up to this morning, or at least some of it?"

Hank, mid-thirties with too much hair combed to one side, took out a pad and a pencil and hailed the bus boy to ask for a telephone. Jesus, Alan thought, only in Hollywood.

Hank hung up and nodded to Mel. "We can start the casting at eleven."

"I suppose somebody is going to have something crazy for breakfast," Alan said, smiling as he looked at the Beverly Hills' breakfast menu with its unorthodox list of steaks, an obscure variety of pear, and omelets with funny-sounding names. He scanned the table to see what the others had ordered so far. He liked the way they served the tomato juice with the half-lemon wrapped in cheesecloth.

"Alan, I've got some surprises for you in the casting session." Mel said it with a devilish look in his eye. He was up to something.

"Really?" Alan took a sip of his small, fluted glass of fresh-squeezed California orange juice, his favorite. He hoped that whatever Mel was conjuring up, he wouldn't discuss it in front of these three production people. He wanted to keep things business-like. But Mel was one of those New Yorkers who had been seduced by the coast and its ways. He loved to feign being a local, "entertaining" out-of-towners for wild evenings among the Polynesian palms at the Luau or wherever the latest night club scene was on the Strip.

Mel smiled at him and winked. The son-of-a-bitch has me fixed up with somebody, he thought to himself.

* * *

Ten o'clock. Alan parked in a reserved space and went into the administration building at Filmgems. He walked past the bust of the Columbia Studio chief and reputed tyrant, Harry Cohn, in the foyer.

He asked the girl behind the glass for directions to the casting session. Except for the skimpy black-and-white getup and the red hair, she was a dead ringer for Liz Taylor's Cleopatra. A phone line buzzed. She turned away to pick up the call, inserted a plug in a hole, and when the tiny light went out, turned back to Alan and indicated a door across the hall and down a few steps.

Motion picture studio offices were really crummy places, Alan thought. Nothing like the movies about the movies. The décor was all 1939 New York World's Fair, complete with ridiculous oversized metal doorknobs.

He entered what appeared to be an executive office. A tall, gray-haired man in a suit was talking on the phone behind the desk. It was the first suit Alan had seen since he'd arrived. Mel was seated on a sofa holding up a photostat of a storyboard and talking to the production manager—what was the guy's name?—whom Alan had met that morning. Two other men were talking by the window.

"Good morning, everybody," Alan called cheerfully.

"Hi, A!" Mel said, getting up and striding over to shake his hand even though they had just had breakfast together. "I want you to meet some of the people who we'll be working with on the shoot."

Mel made introductions. Everyone but the guy at the desk wore the same type of sloppy, puffy, cardigan sweaters Alan had seen at breakfast. With bleached hair and tans they all looked as though they'd been living outdoors most of their lives. Of course, they had.

"We're waiting for the first girls to show up, Alan," Mel continued.

The man in the suit finally got off the phone. He came around and put out his hand.

"Alan, I'm Mike Butler. Nice to have you working with us." Butler was the president of Filmgems.

"Well, Mike, you people do excellent work. I'm glad to get a chance to do something with you. I saw your reel back in New York, and I thought it was excellent."

"That's good. We have virtually the same people working on your job."

Alan hoped this was not just part of the script. These days the changeover in personnel was extraordinary. A young director would shoot half a dozen commercials and suddenly he'd be off doing a feature film.

The buzzer on Butler's desk buzzed.

"That's the first girl." Mel was on his feet again.

Here we go, thought Alan. The door opened, and a tall blonde in a pale-blue willowy dress walked in. She had long legs and pale blue eyes. She carried a white wicker handbag in one hand and a blue leather portfolio in the other. Mel took the portfolio.

"Dear," Mel began. Alan felt a pain of embarrassment.

"It's not important that you meet everybody; you'll forget their names. I just want you to meet two people." Mel turned and pointed to Alan. "This is *the man*, Alan Robinson. He's in charge."

Alan flushed. What a bastard.

"Hi, I'm Pamela Goddard," she said, extending her hand.

"Hi, Pamela."

"And Pamela, this is our director, Geoff Timon."

Geoff was a handsome fellow. He had soft blue eyes—curiously almost the same color as Pamela's—long blonde-gray hair, and an almost-genuine smile. When he spoke, his voice purred like Paul Newman's. Alan had heard him called the best "people director" in the TV commercial business.

Alan asked to look at the girl's portfolio. This was just an act. What everyone in the room was really doing was looking at the girl. Was she right? And after looking at nineteen more actresses, would the men in the room be able to come to a decision?

Over the next hour and a half, eight other beauties came through. Each completed the interview, picked up her portfolio, and swung out the door.

At eleven thirty there was a pause in the action. He felt the energy of his first morning on Pacific time seeping away.

Mel must have noticed. He walked over with a cup of coffee.

"Alan, there's one gal coming over today that I simply know you're going to pick for the older gal's part."

"What's her name?"

"I'm not going to tell you. I want to see if I know you well enough." He grinned and turned away to shuffle through his piles of photographs. Alan remembered the winks at breakfast and felt a wave of dread.

"Can't we do this in sequence, Mel? It's going to get a little confusing if we have one older, then one younger. I can't remember one face from another, let alone going from one part to another."

"It's just the way they're coming in, Alan." Mike, the president of Filmgems, who had been writing at his desk, looked up to answer. "Some of these girls are coming from other studios or all the way from home, and a lot of them live in the Valley."

"Okay. But next time, Mel, when we have more than one role, let's organize things a little better."

"All right, Alan." Mel reddened a bit. Alan had chided him in front of a group of professional motion picture–makers. Mel was an advertising agency producer, one big notch below being a real moviemaker. Alan was an ex-writer who was hoping to make creative director.

Alan guessed what he was thinking.

"I'm sorry, Mel. I didn't know there were problems getting here for the casting call," he said to mollify things. But, he thought, what a sloppy planning job! Mel was the agency's producer. Should I be worried?

Alan was sure the sudden awkward chill would warm when the next girl walked in. She would be stunning, of course. A model trying to become a star. Alan wondered what type of woman Mel thought he would go for. Could he read him that well?

Alan picked up a copy of *The Hollywood Reporter*. He let himself sink into the leather couch. After a few minutes of reading, he couldn't fight the effects of the heavy drone of central air conditioning and closed his eyes.

* * *

At this moment, reader, Alan falls asleep and begins to dream, a plot device that allows me to include material (written by the original author) that may or may not inform the plot—you will be the judge—and that otherwise, (sadly) would have been omitted.

14

The buzzer sounded for number nine. The office door creaked, and Alan looked up from *The Hollywood Reporter* and froze. She looked at the men by the window first.

If this was a joke… but he didn't have the time to form the thought. Mel had leapt up as if to repeat his earlier performance but stopped as he reached her. He took her arm.

She was more beautiful than ever. No hair spray, real pearls.

"Miss Whitman, dear, I'd like to introduce you to the man. This is Alan Robinson. Alan, Claire Whitman is trying out for the second gal's part."

Her smile was all pretenses, but she held his gaze for a moment. Was she surprised? How did she want this to go? Alan managed a smile, and Mel ushered her over to the director.

Jesus, Alan thought. What does she want me to do?

The portfolio was opened, and all the men in the room gathered around Mel as he flipped through the acetate-covered pictures. The photographs of Claire were set against nineteenth-century mansions, racing stables, Victorian beach clubs, and other symbols of elegance. Alan gazed at the photo retrospective of the girl standing beside him, the girl writer he had last seen beneath the awning of 554 West 110th Street. He recognized the perfume. Her Bergdorf first-floor scent.

Mel rattled on, asking the availability and the conflict questions.

"Have you seen a script?" he continued.

"Yes, my agent sent me a copy."

"How does it feel?"

"All right. I'm the older gal, I assume."

"Yes."

"Then the script is fine. I think it's a cute idea."

"Okay, thanks. We'll be in touch…"

Claire reached for her portfolio and turned to go.

"Excuse me," Alan interrupted. "Where do you shop for your groceries?"

Claire turned slowly, took a step toward him, cocked her head to one side, and took his bait with a wily smile.

"A&P of course."

Alan nodded his head dumbly.

After the door had closed, Mel gave Alan a panicked look. The ad was for Lucky Stores; Alan usually insisted on authentic brand loyalty.

"Do we have to wait for the next ten?" Alan said smiling.

"You like?"

"Fabulous."

"That's the one, Alan! I knew you'd dig her. Was I right or what?"

An hour later, after the last girl had closed the door, Mel Fox rose out of his chair holding a piece of paper and a ballpoint pen.

"Everybody completed their ballots?"

"Let's go to lunch," somebody said. It was Mike Butler, the president.

"Where do you want to go, Alan?"

"I don't care. Any place that's close." He needed to get away, figure out what had just happened, why Claire was in California. Had she known he would be on this business? She couldn't have. Had he even told her about the trip? He couldn't remember. He'd get through lunch and then find an excuse to go back to the hotel.

"Okay, let's go to the Derby." Mel folded his copy of the storyboard and jammed it into his blue jeans.

Damn, was Mel trying to make it up to him or was he just trying to outdo Butler? The Brown Derby was one of Hollywood's last famous landmarks in what Alan called "the old Hollywood."

"It may be hard to get in at this time," Butler said, taking a pack of cigarettes from his desk and tucking them into his suit coat pocket, "but we'll give it a whirl."

Alan looked out the window. It was one o'clock, and the sun blazed. He felt instinctively for his sunglasses. If you walked out into that glare, you'd probably be blinded for ten minutes.

The streets were lined with ten- and twelve-story vintage office buildings separated by alleyways and marred by the occasional Whalen's Drugstore. The corner of Hollywood and Vine, the crossroads of show business, looked a lot like 5th and Sycamore in Cincinnati: unremarkable. Yet, only a few buildings down the block from that corner, one couldn't miss the Brown Derby, unchanged since the thirties, a genuine star hangout.

After turning Butler's Lincoln Continental over to a parking lot attendant, Alan, Butler, Mel, and Geoff Timon walked in the back entrance that lead to the lounge. The restaurant was divided: two-thirds main dining room and the rest a long, narrow bar and lounge. Caricatures of Hollywood celebrities—all in the same style—covered the walls. They reminded Alan of the caricatures of members of his fraternity done by itinerant artists who visited college campuses in the forties.

Butler walked past the bar and through the archway that led to the main dining room. Alan followed; still, after all these years, a hopeless stargazer. Mel had fallen behind. While Butler shook hands with the maître d, Alan scanned the dining room. Every banquette and table were occupied. He spotted Phil Harris and Bing Crosby at the table nearest the entrance. Phil Silvers was halfway down the same side of the restaurant at a huge table with Harvey Lembeck—the comedian and song-and-dance man who had saved the *Beach Party* movies with his Eric Von Zipper character—and three lesser businessmen all wearing black silk suits. Agents, Alan thought. The actor who played the lead in *Twelve O'Clock High* was talking to one of the members of his bomber crew. Pretty good turnout.

Butler turned. "We're dead."

"How long a wait?"

"Thirty minutes at least."

"The hell with it," Alan said. "I think I'll just go back to the hotel and crap out." He really wanted to get away from everybody. He was still jet-lagged from the trip, and now he needed to figure out how to reach Claire.

After seeing half a dozen people, casting sessions became a blur. Handsome young actors and actresses all looked alike. But what a shocker seeing Claire here surrounded by all this phoniness. Alan picked up his briefcase to follow Butler and the rest back out to the car. Having decided on another lunch venue, they dropped Alan back at Filmgems.

"Tomorrow morning then, nine o'clock?" Alan climbed out of the Lincoln.

"That's it, Alan. Have a good day." Butler lowered the automatic window from the driver's side, and Alan leaned in and shook his hand.

He doesn't give a damn whether I have a good day or a good evening or a good anything, Alan thought as he walked across the parking lot. I am just another New York agency guy he's glad he doesn't have to entertain.

Alan climbed into his parked rental and started it up. He swung the car onto Sunset Boulevard by the New York Life Insurance Company Building. With the windows down—he hadn't rented a convertible—the car quickly cooled. He turned on the radio to *KBIG*, the only jazz station in Southern California. Why was America's show business capitol so lacking in good jazz? After the Lighthouse and Shelly's Manne-Hole, the club on North Cahuenga Boulevard, there was nothing much to look at.

He drove along the curvy part of Sunset Boulevard again, past Dino's with the big neon die-cut of Dean Martin staring vacantly over the terrace in front of the building. He passed the new Playboy Club. "Just a lot of Prudential Insurance salesmen," Wally had once said.

He got into the left-hand turn lane at Doheny Avenue, and when the traffic thinned ahead of him, he shot down the hill. He saw a Lucky supermarket and swung in. Usually on the first day on the coast he would buy a ninety-nine-cent Styrofoam ice bucket, a bag of ice, and a six-pack of Coors Beer. He would take the beer back to his room at the Beverly Hills Hotel, go out the sliding glass doors to the small ivy-walled patio, turn on the radio, and drink. "Welcome to Hollywood."

But instead, today he would put a bottle of wine in his basket because today, when he got back to the hotel, he would make a phone call.

Claire Whitman! Trying out for the part of the older gal in the Lucky's commercial. How did that happen? What was it about her? He'd jotted down her contact number. He was sure she'd be waiting for his call.

* * *

Early in the morning a few days later no other guests had joined them yet on the pool deck at the Beverly Hills Hotel. Alan squinted. Across the pool, Claire appeared to have nothing on. He watched her climb out of the water—so unlike Lina—and he wanted her more.

But since eight thirty Claire had been full of questions, acting like his student. It was exasperating. She approached their glass-topped table now, rubbing her dripping hair with the hotel towel. "You didn't tell me why you work on existing brands. I would think a man like you would like chasing new business."

"Your coffee is cold."

"That's okay, thank you. I've had enough." She sat and extended her legs in the direction of the sun. "I want to learn everything I can. I mean it. Tell me your story, Alan.

"My story." Alan looked at his watch. "You know you have to be at the shoot at eleven."

"That's why I got here so early—so we would have time. And so I could use your pool." Her eyes danced when she smiled.

In his private fantasy, they had had a tumbling, whispering night of lovemaking. Obviously that didn't happen, but she was here, wasn't she? Right in front of him.

"When we were driving along Mulholland Drive the other evening, you said something about hating to make presentations. Is that why you avoid new business? Because you don't like the pitch?"

"Claire! Are you interviewing me?"

"What?" She giggled. "Maybe. I want to know! Hasn't anyone asked you these things before?"

"All I want to do is look at you."

"I will not be seduced, Mister Prettywords. Well, maybe." She slid down her dark glasses and smiled at him. "Please tell me."

"Sure. Yes, I hate making presentations. New business presentations especially. You put your best ideas out there, and in minutes your work is dismissed by a couple of insecure company directors. In the trash. With existing clients, at least one has the context, the history. It's not as, um, dangerous." This felt awkward.

"So, copywriters aren't insulated from all that?"

"Not once they get into management. Taking crap from the client is pretty central. It's part of the business. I wish I liked it more. I mean, the pitch. Lately I wish I liked the business more." For a moment all they heard was the murmur of the pool pumps.

Suddenly Alan sat up.

"Christ! Claire, you need to shower if you are going to make it. You forget, I am in charge."

She was up in a single movement. The bikini disappearing as she wrapped the towel around her. Then, facing him, she smiled. Who did she remind him of?

"So, why do you do it, Alan? You are young. If you aren't happy where you are, make a change."

And with that, she retreated to the dressing room, and he was left to consider the shadows of the early morning.

He got up and felt in his pocket for his key. A large black crow landed on the deserted poolside bar. Alan watched it for a minute, thinking to himself: if it were only that simple.

15

Alan stood by the picture window in his office and looked at the New York skyline. He'd been back for a week from a five-day trip to the coast. Nothing was quite as it had been.

He gazed at the view through late-afternoon beams of orange sun, and for a moment he was distracted from his work day. It seemed a new building appeared every week where before there had been a block of shabby five-story buildings. As Midtown transformed, the neighborhood stores were all going. His favorite Irish bar with the steam table, the camera store that sold cheap film. The fruit and vegetable stores were vanishing downtown below 60th. He stared out the window, but the view faded. His mind returned to the upcoming weekend working on the Jamesville new soup account. His felt his stomach churn.

Why was his team being called in? He usually worked on new pitches for old brands, familiar clients, not new product development for new clients. The agency had done the product testing for this new Jamesville line, Wholesome Soup, a not-from-concentrate rival of the major brand. The stuff had done so well it was going to national distribution. Now Dunaway was trying like mad to get the business. So, why his group?

"Alan." Bob Howe, the agency president, was on the phone that morning. "Alan, we have one heck of an opportunity on the Jamesville Wholesome Soup business. I met with the Jamesville people today and got the nod. We have a real chance to land this account. This could mean Dunaway takes the rest of Jamesville Foods."

Alan smiled and nodded as he listened.

"Is this the end of détente with Baker and Dodge? I thought they had the pickles and the rest of Jamesville's older brands."

Howe adjusted his approach. "Not at all. We aren't after any of their existing brands. We want the new business and future new business. So, are you up for this? Three weeks. A real concerted effort. It's really a fantastic opportunity, and we'd like you to help."

Sound upbeat, he told himself. Team player.

"I'd love to, Bob. Can I get some information from the account group?"

"Well, we're having a briefing Saturday morning."

"Saturday." Neutral voice. Keep it neutral.

"We thought it would be better if we worked without any distractions. You know, the telephone, other clients." Howe's voice had lost some of its confidence.

"I assume you want me to have some of my people in this briefing?"

"Your people and Tom Hartley's." The voice was suddenly serious.

"Bob, may I ask you a somewhat direct question?" Of course, he couldn't ask the obvious question: had the latest campaign pitch fallen flat?

"Shoot."

"Is the product for real? Is it competitive?"

"Come on, Alan, of course it is. Dunaway did the research! And now we want to put our best talent on this project." Alan held the phone away and looked at it as though Bob Howe was sitting inside the receiver.

Something didn't feel right. Shifting personnel midstream wasn't that unusual, but bringing in two groups to work together on a new product campaign was. This was a push.

There went the weekend.

"Okay, Bob. Whatever you say. I'll have half a dozen people here at nine Saturday morning."

"Good, Alan. Appreciate it."

"Incidentally, Bob, how do you get into this place on Saturdays?"

"Don't worry, we'll have someone downstairs. Just ask your people to have their I.D. cards. And, incidentally, we'll have plenty of beer and sandwiches and stuff from The Stage Delicatessen."

"Swell." Alan had to admit he liked their stuffed sandwiches.

The call with Howe made clear everything he didn't want to admit about big agencies—everything Wally and others had repeatedly claimed to justify their career moves. Why would you work for the man when you could call the shots yourself? The president and his aides gave orders and expected no questions. Fifteen percent commission; that's all that mattered. Timing had no bearing on anything. Family. Weekends. All secondary.

It troubled him, his waning faith in those in charge. More so ever since that push on the coffee campaign last year, when he and Joe Hurley, head of research, had joked at lunch. Hurley had been about to eat a little neck clam. He held the clam above in the little glass cup and then submerged it in the cocktail sauce. He had looked at Alan with a flat expression and said, "Alan. Remember. It's a master-slave relationship."

Now, Alan turned and sat down at his desk and stared at the color photograph of his two boys. "The swim meet is Saturday; they won't even notice. But sailing, who can I get to help them rig?" He was talking out loud to himself.

"Losing your grip, Alan?" Charlie Ogden stood in the doorway with a layout pad and his pipe drooping out of his mouth. "You know when you start talking to yourself—"

Alan stood and turned around. "You're going to be talking to yourself too, old friend. You're working this weekend."

"My ass, I am."

"Your ass you are. There's a push on the new Wholesome Soup business, and the president of the agency has asked me to help out. The briefing is tomorrow. Saturday."

"Oh, come on," Charlie said, sinking onto the two-seater sofa opposite Alan's desk. "Christ, the summer's short enough as it is."

"Sorry, man. I'm staying too. And so are all the people. You better tell them."

"What a shitty business."

Charlie got up and walked out. Alan knew the bitching was real, but he'd be at the agency on time, come Saturday.

Alan looked at his watch. In half an hour the five-fifteen train to the country would leave Grand Central, and he wouldn't be on it.

* * *

Mid-morning on Tuesday Alan sat around with his people in Tom's office. They'd worked the weekend. The graphic designer got up and excused himself, carrying the notes and the latest sketches for their "freshly made" soup pitch for Jamesville's Wholesome Soup. Now Alan, Charlie, and Tom could laugh about the night before at PJs.

Tom's phone rang.

"Tom Hartley." Tom's response was automatic and businesslike. Then he broke into a big grin.

"Hi, Hugh! We missed you last night. Just talking about it. Not too late. About one, I guess. An awful lot of wine."

Tom held the phone receiver to his ear, listening. He nodded. Then nodded again.

"Sure. Come on over. I didn't make the bed though. I was late as hell this morning."

Tom nodded at the phone again. "No problem. See ya."

He hung up.

"A certain buddy of mine wants to use my apartment for a nooner."

"Lucky bastard," Charlie muttered.

"You do that sort of thing, Charlie?" Alan asked. "I thought that was strictly a married man's scene."

"Are you kidding? It's us young guys the secretaries really like, Alan, not you old cats."

"Who's the chick, Tom? Do you know her?"

Tom nodded.

"Fabulous girl. She's a Czech. And believe it or not, she's an account executive at an agency. Very hip. One time we were at this Japanese restaurant and Hugh says something funny, and Tori—that's her name, Tori—takes him by the shoulders, kisses him, and then turns to me and says, 'I just love married bachelors!' How about that? Married bachelors!"

"That's hip, alright." Alan muttered. He'd had enough.

"So, where are we going for lunch?" Charlie asked, looking at his brightly colored, round watch.

Alan got up. He wasn't going to stick around for this conversation: agency men could never decide where to go for lunch.

At that moment the phone rang again.

"Tom Hartley." He smiled, but the delivery was just as before. "Sure, send him in." Tom dropped the phone into the cradle.

"That's Hugh," Tom said, lowering his voice and gesturing to them to be quiet. "He's here for my keys. For Chrissakes, don't act like you know what's up."

Hugh walked into Tom's office. He was grinning and carrying a paper grocery bag.

"What's in the bag, Hugh?" Charlie tried to sound bored.

"Cold shrimp and a bottle of wine," Hugh replied, holding out his hand for the apartment keys.

"You got a nooner?" Alan asked, now that the shrimp and cold wine were in evidence.

"A little exercise, some cold shrimp, a bottle of Pouilly Fuissé, and a couple of Sinatra records," Hugh said smiling. "Thanks, man."

There was an awkward silence as he spun out the door. For a moment they were a group of thirteen-year-old boys with no idea how to get a date.

"So, Dewey's?" asked Alan. He'd only been once this week.

"Sure. Give me five minutes," answered Tom.

16

"**I** think they're trying to screw us," Alan snarled as he got into the limousine.

"Who?" Bob Wilson, the account management supervisor, asked. Alan and Wilson had just finished presenting the new advertising for Wholesome Soups to Jamesville's account reps. The presentation had bombed. Alan was flummoxed.

"Baker and Dodge. Those bastards have already been up here trying to get this business. I'll bet anything!" replied Alan.

Baker had the bulk of Jamesville's advertising and, as far as Alan knew, Dunaway was trying to develop the new soup brand—that was their thing. They weren't about stealing any established accounts. At least that's what the agency president had told him at the start of this whole thing.

Alan was beginning to see it. Of course Baker and Dodge wanted the new products, too! That's where the money was, not in old brands.

Jamesville had assigned the test product to Dunaway. It had done so well it was going into national distribution, and Dunaway, among other agencies, had a shot at building the brand. This would be the perfect time for the president of ad-maker, Baker and Dodge, to call the president of food giant, Jamesville, and say, "Well, Bill, now that you've got a brand ready to go national, why don't you assign it to us? We've handled all your major national brands." Logical but underhanded.

"Those bastards," Alan repeated himself as he pressed the button that automatically raised the window beside him—he was fascinated

82

with limousine push-button windows. Maniacally he began to make the window go up and down, up and down. It helped him think.

"You don't know for sure, Alan," Bob Wilson responded weakly. His thin face had become more sallow than usual. Bob had been in charge of long time consumer food accounts at Dunaway. He was a safe-business sort of guy. Might have been in life insurance if his father hadn't pulled some strings back in the '50s.

"You can bet I'm going to find out." Alan was still fooling with the window. "It's time to do a little triangulation."

"What do you mean?"

"Well, when you want to know what's really going on, you ask two different guys from two different agencies or companies and see if what they say jibes with what you think. You know bloody goddamn well this town isn't very big as far as gossip and shit is concerned."

"What are you saying?" Wilson fumbled, trying to unbutton his collar. He looked as if he couldn't breathe.

"I'm going to spy."

"Jesus Christ, has it come to that?"

"Maybe spy is too dramatic a word, but I'll bet within a week I'll know if those fuckers are after the business. Then we can do something about it."

"What?"

"I don't know, but something. Maybe just go and tell the client to stop playing games."

"You can't do that!"

"Ever try?"

"No."

"Well, then." Alan's anger had found a purpose. It helped that he had Wilson's rapt attention. Then it dawned on him.

"The first thing I'm going to do is call a buddy of mine at Pando McCabe and see what he knows. Then I'm going to talk to the guys at Brother Rat's."

"What'll that accomplish?"

"Are you kidding? The bar at Brother Rat's is where suppliers hang out. Editors, music reps, production people, freelance directors. If Baker is doing a speculative presentation for the client, one of those cats will know."

"Aren't there security procedures for something like this?" Wilson had a point. A lot of agency and corporate presidents did have written security procedures. They even ordered CONFIDENTIAL stamps from Goldsmith's, not that that did any good.

"Security, my ass. Take a walk through the editing floor of any of the production houses like EUE (Screen Gems) and you can pretty much find out who will be doing what in the next six months."

"Really?" Bob asked. He was thinking of the security of his own brands.

"Want another source? Walk around MediaSound or Aura or National Recording and just listen, man. You'll hear the tracks for the commercials while they're being recorded."

"Don't they have closed sets?"

"Nope. If you want to be really sneaky, you could just dress like a slob and bring in a handful of coffee containers to any stage or studio and ask who ordered the coffee."

"You wouldn't…"

The limousine stopped. They had reached the agency.

"I'll call Bill Taylor as soon as we get upstairs. He knows everybody. Want to come see what happens?"

Alan and Bob went up the private elevator to the 33rd floor. As the door opened, Alan took off his jacket and threw it over his shoulder. He felt pretty good. Jazzed up.

He gestured to Bob.

"After you."

* * *

They entered the creative department through the enormous leather-padded doorway. Alan smiled at the four typing secretaries arranged in a four-stall cubicle. Frederick Taylor meet Herman Miller, he thought. They reached the corner of the floor, Alan's office.

"Any messages, Doris?"

"No, Alan."

"Thank God."

Loosening his tie with one hand, he dialed Bill, the friend who'd invited him to judge the Gold Letter Awards this year, with the other. Before Bill had helped start Pando McCabe, a small agency that was making it big, he had spent a few years at Baker and Dodge. Bill was his first source for triangulating what was up with the Wholesome Soup account.

"Is he in?"

"No. I'm sorry," replied a girl on the other end of the phone. "He just stepped away from his desk."

Alan rolled his eyes and smiled. Stepped away from his desk? Did Bill have an office half the size of Madison Square Garden?

"Well, when he gets back to his desk, ask him to call Alan Robinson, please." Alan hung up. He sat down on the two-seater sofa opposite his own desk and threw his tie and jacket over the coffee table.

"You know, Bob, I rarely get this emotional about things, really—"

The phone rang.

Alan grabbed the phone on the windowsill next to his enormous dictionary.

"Alan Robinson."

"Alan?" The voice on the phone made Alan smile.

"Bill? How are you, man?"

"Great. How about yourself?"

"Well, reasonably well, William. But I've got a problem. Maybe you can help. I think your old agency is doing a number on my agency."

"How so?"

"Do you know anything about the..."

"You mean the soup thing?"

Alan shook his head and looked at Bob Wilson. Wilson's eyes grew wider and a little frightened-looking.

"I mean the soup thing. You know about it! Is Baker really going after it?"

"What do you think? Wouldn't you?"

"Jesus, Bill, I don't think so. Good God, Wholesome is supposed to be a multi-agency outfit. Baker has business: we have business. That's the whole idea."

"Sure, Alan," Bill said knowingly, sarcastically.

"Well, what's the story?"

"I don't know for sure. You didn't hear it from me, but Baker and Dodge made a presentation to somebody over there. That's the way they work. It was all above board."

I'll bet I know how they did it too, Alan thought. Probably gave them some kind of a "here's-how-we-see-you-in-the-future" bullshit, and our brands were part of the presentation.

"Don't get over-excited about it," Bill continued, "but you might want to rally the troops. I'll bet they did a shitpot full of their own research."

"Christ." Alan sunk in the sofa. "I swear, Bill, we know this brand, and we know who's using the stuff. We've been on a huge push. I can't think of a thing we haven't tried, tested, and tossed. No shit."

"Well, what do you want me to do?"

"Find out who they presented to. How they did it. On film, concept boards, animatics. Anything, so I can find out what they did, okay?"

"Thy will be done."

"When will you know something?"

"Oh, by noon tomorrow, probably."

Alan cupped the speaking part of the telephone and grinned at Bob. "By noon tomorrow. Is that soon enough?" he asked Bob.

Bob nodded his head, as he lit a cigarette. "What a great business," he muttered to himself.

"Hey man, Bill, I can't thank you enough," Alan said into the phone.

"Oh, yes you can. I'll talk to you tomorrow. Incidentally, I wouldn't sweat it. There are a lot of guys at Wholesome who can't stand Baker. This I know."

"Well then, I hope this little tactic backfires on those bastards."

"I think it will. No shit."

"Okay, old friend, I'll talk to you tomorrow."

Alan hung up. Bob Wilson looked even paler than he had a few minutes ago.

"Bob?"

Wilson looked up.

"You smoke too much."

"Yeah, that's what my kids say. So, what's the story?"

Alan smiled confidently for the first time since his doomed presentation.

"Bob, I wouldn't worry."

17

New York's Racquet and Tennis Club stood grandly, covering a full block on Park Avenue. Alan passed through the marble lobby, glancing at the ugly oversized statue of the tennis player. Upstairs in the large ornate bar on the second floor he looked around for Giff Norman. Gray and balding men posed here and there playing board games, shaking dice. The room opened to the dining room. Giff, a short man with black hair and noticeably fit, stood and offered his hand when he saw Alan.

Alan had thought about joining the Racquet and Tennis Club. The location was perfect for meeting clients like this. He had admired the squash and tennis courts on the top floor which were illuminated like a museum by huge skylights.

Then he had looked at the membership directory; not one committee member worked Midtown. All their telephone numbers had the familiar "Rector" exchange prefix indicating addresses downtown: Wall Street, the banks and brokerage houses. (In 1967 New York was divided into telephone exchanges, Trafalgar (TR), Murry Hill (MU), etc.) So, even though it was cheaper than the University Club, the Racquet was not an option for Alan, the copywriter.

Giff Norman had suggested the Racquet when Alan had called him about the Wholesome Soup account. He knew Giff from years ago when Giff had been on the agency side. Alan thought he could reason with him, at least get him to go back to Wholesome management and raise a doubt about the Baker and Dodge tactics.

Was Giff like the dozen or so agency account people Alan knew who had crossed over? Any really good agency man—someone who thought strategically, took risks—stayed on the agency side. Giff, who worked for Jamesville, might be the exception, but Alan didn't know him well enough to know. Before the soup ad presentation the other day, they'd only met at a couple of studio jam sessions where Giff had played drums to Alan's keyboards.

Alan hoped that calling Giff directly—assuring him personally that Dunaway was the only agency for this new business—would pay off. Otherwise, they were all in the toilet. Someone at Dunaway would lose his job.

Alan had hatched his "venal scheme" on the day of the presentation. As promised, Bill Taylor had talked to insiders and production people about the Baker and Dodge campaign. The scouting had yielded plenty: they wanted the business. And now the higher-ups at Dunaway were appearing to back off, lighten up, like they were assuming the business was theirs. In his confusion he called Giff, Jamesville Foods advertising accounts manager. Giff had presumably seen Baker's presentation as well as Dunaway's. When he agreed to have lunch, Alan knew there was hope.

The dining room at the Racquet Club hummed with male voices making deals and comparing portfolios. Alan saw it all around him, feigned indifference and veiled rudeness. Pungent blue smoke hung in the air.

The meal was predictable. Like the last time Alan had lunched there, the *plat du jour* was roast leg of lamb with mint jelly.

Alan got to the point.

"So, Giff. You know the facts. Dunaway did the research and has the track record. We tested the message on homemakers in three states for you and they loved it. They loved the product too. You make the call and you're the man. I'm telling you."

Giff remained surprisingly vague and indecisive. As Alan had feared, a typical company account man.

"Well, Alan, I would need to figure out how to go about this. I thought Dunaway's presentation was flawless, but I don't make the decisions. Like I said, I have not heard back. There may be factors beyond my control." Giff poured a cream substitute into his coffee cup. The coffee turned almost white.

"What does that mean?" Now Alan was worried.

"You know how it is. There are many dimensions to this."

"Dimensions? Let's start with the selling soup dimension. You've got to know your soup-making friends in Camden—Campbell Soups—are thinking up the next big thing right now. Chunkier, meatier. Hell, maybe soup that makes you lose weight! In fact, I'll bet the Burnett—Leo Burnett Worldwide—guys are on their way to that big gray building right now."

"Alan, don't lose your cool."

"I'm sorry. I must be missing something. I thought with a new product like this one, the sooner it goes live the better." Alan ate the olive from his martini before the waiter whisked it away. Giff ordered the cheesecake.

It was true, Alan thought. He was losing his cool. It didn't help anything to care too much.

They chatted for a few minutes about the New York Giants terrible last season. It was clear Giff didn't want to talk about business.

"Like a cigar, Alan?"

"No, Giff. Thanks." He tried to smile, but the smell turned his stomach. "I have to get back."

"Don't you agency guys still take long lunches?"

Alan restrained himself in his retort; he was trying not to think of Giff as the typical corporate man.

"It's two ten," he replied. "We all should be getting back."

They walked down the stairs together to the ornate Racquet Club lobby. Little men with RC insignia on their jackets were helping big men with their coats.

Alan tried to be jovial. "Next time on me, Giff. My dining room's prettier than your dining room—although the food is about the same."

Giff stopped in the middle of having his raincoat put on. Alan sensed something amiss with the balance of power.

"You belong to a club?" Giff's look could have been benign amusement or bemused incredulity, Alan wasn't sure, but he knew how social exclusion worked. This guy was thinking, "Alan Robinson, the self-made copywriter, has a club in New York?"

For a moment Alan felt that dreaded inner heat, something like humiliation mixed with panic that came upon him when he doubted himself, realized he might not belong. Giff Norman is just another asshole, he told himself, but you need this guy.

"Yes, I belong to the University Club." He threw back as casually as he could. "I'm also in the *Social Register*."

They walked out into the bright sun. The rain had stopped. The raincoats were superfluous and hot.

"Giff, it would be great if Dunaway could help you guys at Jamesville launch this thing," Alan said, choosing his words. He felt back on top. "With us, you have everything you need to go ahead. The product. The people. The advertising. Jamesville has an opportunity to be first. First! When was the last time you guys were first in the market place? And you, sir, could be a goddamn hero besides."

Taking their raincoats off, they both attempted to shake hands and say goodbye. It was a funny scene. Alan had half a raincoat on. Giff had his off already, draped over his hand-shaking arm. In a fumble of Brooks Brothers raincoats, the client and the agency parted from each other.

18

The following Thursday night Alan needed a break; for two days the Dunaway group had been reworking the Jamesville campaign. He needed to get his head out of the agency for a while, but everybody he knew fled the city early in August. Who would be around? Who was in the city all the time? He reached for a Chiclet and started to chew.

What about Buffy Collins? That's it, he thought. Buffy worked in an art gallery in Midtown. She had to be here on Thursdays, unless the galleries all moved to the Hamptons for the summer. It was worth a try.

Alan got out his telephone directory. I wonder if she's still listed under her married name or by her maiden name again? And what does Buffy stand for? He'd never known her given name.

"Doris, would you get the Sumner Gallery on the phone for me? Ask for Buffy Collins." Alan smiled. Maybe this would improve his week. He hadn't heard from Claire, and Liddie was talking about coming back early to shop for school clothes.

Buffy and Alan had met in Dallas four years ago when he was shooting some commercials with the Dallas Cowboys. She was the public relations director for a big hotel there. Alan had met her through a sportswriter on the *Dallas Star*, a friend of a friend. Buffy Collins knew everybody in Dallas, and maybe she could show Alan the town? Their dinners had broken up the monotony of several short trips to that awful city.

Then, last summer, she had come to New York and Alan had taken her out.

Doris had the Sumner Gallery on the phone.

"Buffy?"

"Yes."

"It's Alan Robinson."

"My God! Alan, how are you?"

"Fine."

"It's Thursday night; aren't you supposed to be on your way to the country?" Buffy knew all there was to know about Alan's summer lifestyle. "As a matter of fact, how come you haven't called me yet this summer, you rat?"

"Well, I heard you were going with some English baron or something."

"Oh Alan, that's just a weekend in the Hamptons now and then. I'm not involved with anybody. At least not seriously."

"Well, that's why I called. I thought maybe you'd like to have dinner with me tonight. I'm stuck in town trying to save an account." Alan noticed a pause before Buffy responded.

"Are you by any chance working on something for Jamesville Foods?" Buffy's voice was cool and flat.

Alan looked at the phone. Now, how in hell does she know I'm working on the Wholesome Soup push?

"What are you, clairvoyant or something? How…?"

"Don't bother, Alan. Go to Pequot tonight. The account is going to Baker and Dodge."

"What do you mean?" Alan couldn't get a sensible question formed in his mind.

"I can't tell you how I know, Alan, but the account is going to go to the Baker and Dodge Agency. It is. I mean, I really know it is."

Alan took a deep breath in and out.

"Well. This is certainly bizarre. Would you like to have dinner anyway?" Keep it cool, he told himself.

"I can't tonight. But I will have a drink with you."

"All right. Where's your gallery?"

"Fifty-seventh and Madison."

"I'll meet you at the Saint Regis in three minutes," he said and managed to laugh. "I meant this to be purely social, but I will use all the means at my disposal to get you to tell me absolutely everything."

"Looking forward to it, but like I said… Anyway, see you shortly."

Alan hung up. He looked out the window again for the thousandth time. What was going on?

His watch said ten past five. Bob Howe would have left by now to catch a daylight savings time round of golf at Round Hill. He'd have to tell Howe in the morning during the briefing.

He put on a pair of sunglasses, shut the light off above his desk, and walked out to the elevator.

How does an old flame, who works in an art gallery, just happen to know we're going to lose the Jamesville business, when he hadn't been able figure out what was happening? And why did her name pop into his head to call? Tonight of all nights. Alan shook his head. On the one hand, he didn't care what happened, but on the other hand, he'd busted his ass for Dunaway and his group these past two weeks. If the agency did lose the business, they would fire somebody. Who would it be? Probably Lou, his creative director. But what then?

Alan said goodnight to two paste-up men who were already working on charts for the next Jamesville presentation. Poor bastards, he thought. They work the hardest and they're the last to know.

* * *

Buffy finished her gin and tonic.[7]

"Love, I've got to go. I wish I could do dinner but I just can't. Stay and finish your drink, and I'll talk to you next week." Buffy leaned down and kissed Alan on the cheek.

"It is always great to see you, Buff. And thanks."

Four tables of men on either side of theirs stopped talking as she made an S with her body to get out from behind the table. Man, she's good-looking, Alan thought, and she's shacked up with Charlie Wacker!

Alan waved to the waiter again and gestured with his hands to bring the check.

He wasn't sure what to do. Could he really tell the president of the agency that a girl he knew was sleeping with Charlie Wacker, the president of Baker and Dodge, and that Wacker told her in bed the other night that Baker and Dodge was going to get the new Jamesville Foods Wholesome Soup account? Howe wouldn't believe it, and he'd ask questions Alan wouldn't be able to answer. What was the point of saying anything?

So, they had done all that work, two creative groups, an intense push. What would be next? Go through the motions? He had recognized something was up when he gave the presentation to the Wholesome executives. The company men had said all the right things, but it had seemed phony, unconvincing. So, he had run around trying to get answers. He'd put in his noble effort. What now?

It would be hard to keep silent. But he would if he had to. This was business, and who knew? Maybe somebody would change his mind, he thought. Maybe Wacker was giving Buffy a lot of crap.

The check was $11.50 for four gin and tonics. Jesus, this town is getting expensive.

He peeled a twenty-dollar bill from the small clip of dollars he took from his pocket. Goddamn spy money, he thought.

The waiter came with the change, and Alan got up, tipped the white-coated Italian, and walked briskly out through the crowded doorway into the lobby. The noise in the King Cole Bar faded behind him.

He walked slowly through the lobby, taking in the people sitting by the windows and standing around the cashier's cage and front desk. He inhaled a mixture of perfumes that he could vaguely distinguish. Alan could always spot Shalimar and Magriffe. Small wonder. Lina wore Shalimar and Liddie wore Magriffe.

He bought a copy of the *New York Post*, stepped through the revolving door, and beckoned the doorman to hail a cab.

* * *

Friday, three o'clock.

"Mr. Howe is expecting you." The secretary came from behind her desk and opened the door to the president's office.

Bob Howe, the president of J Dunaway Advertising, placed the phone down as they entered. He rose from his oversized leather chair, a larger-than-life portrait of a trim blonde woman—Howe's wife, Alan recalled—dressed in a sexy green riding habit on the wall behind him.

"Good to see you, Alan!"

They shook hands. Alan started right in with his speech.

"Bob, I'd like to talk to you about the Wholesome Soup campaign. You wanted Tom's and my people working it. You said it wasn't a big push, but we heard you and came up with a visually good-looking campaign directed at the product. The guys did some good work. They gave me everything we needed to score with Jamesville. I presented it Monday."

"I heard it went well. Alan, have a seat. Would you like a coffee, maybe a drink?"

"No, thanks." Alan looked at the chair and sat. This might not go well. "Bob, I've gotten word that Baker and Dodge are making a play for the Wholesome Soup advertising."

"Your sources have it wrong, Alan. I have a phone call with Jamesville first thing tomorrow." Bob's voice sounded like he'd just woken up from a nap. Maybe he needed one; the cap was off the Chivas on the bar in the corner.

"Bob, I heard something from somebody..." Alan continued. Should he mention the presentation? The feeling he had had that the company account guy would rather have been filing his nails than listening to their pitch? That would be a mistake. He would be under-mining his group and Tom's. But what about Buffy's intrigue?

"I appreciate your concern, Alan. I haven't seen the boards myself, but Lou went to South Hampton last night, Alan. That tells me he's pretty confident. The weather is supposed to be nice at the shore."

"Look, Bob..." Go slow. Offer up valuable information. Don't whine.

"I have some information you need. I am speaking in confidence and under oath, you might say—you know how small this town is—but the president of Baker and Dodge told a friend of mine that they had the Wholesome Soup account. Baker has some arrangement. The account is theirs."

Bob Howe fiddled with a pen on his desk, then neatened a sheaf of papers. Alan watched his boss's face for a sign of anger, panic, disappointment, even puzzlement. Instead, Bob smiled, a look of simple pleasure, of satisfaction with life. Was he stoned? Alan was stumped.

"You have given me a lot to think about ahead of my phone call with Jamesville Foods. I appreciate your loyalty to Dunaway, Alan, but let's not say anything more about it."

He paused and sat back, then continued jovially, "Dunaway had a mention this morning in the *Times* for the Lucky Stores advertising. Did you see it? You have a heck of a list of television credits, Alan. We are lucky to have you." With that, he rose.

Alan stood up too. "No, I didn't see it." Who could read the paper with all this on his mind?

"Miss Ames has it on her desk; take a look. And promise me that you will go sailing this weekend."

Alan felt his hands open and close as if they were primed to plead for his job, plead for something! Instead, he said, "Okay. Maybe I'll go to the country too. Make some points with my wife."

There was nothing to do; he'd head to the train by five. Of course, he had to manage his people. What should he tell them? Kudos from the president?

"I'll talk to the writers before I leave. They are taking material to the studio musicians next week."

"Sounds good, Alan."

As he walked out of the office he couldn't help feeling like he had missed a sign on the road or stepped onto the wrong subway platform. Something was amiss. He thanked Bob and closed the door. At the secretary's desk, he saw today's *New York Times.*

"Mind if I look for a clipping?" he asked.

"Be my guest," replied Miss Ames, her steel gray hair pinned up with a navy bow. Alan was well aware that president's secretaries were more like executive assistants: loyal confidantes and occasional company strategists. "Bottom of the column, page eight."

As she handed the newspaper to Alan, he noticed an open folder beside the massive typewriter. The label on the folder said "Walter Hendricks."

Wally?

Alan unfolded the newspaper to the brief listing of new television campaigns. Looking over the top of the paper he saw a partially written memo in the typewriter carriage. He read, "...offer you the position of creative director..."

He realized Miss Ames was talking to him; something about the new mail boy being slow.

"Yes. Right," Alan said, folding the paper and returning it to the desk.

"Thank you, Miss Ames. Goodbye."

"Tell Doris hello."

"Will do." His mind spinning in all directions, he headed for the elevator.

19

The next Wednesday Alan met his friend Bill Taylor at Mullaley's on 1st Avenue. Mullaley's was one of those original Irish bars that managed to keep its anonymity. The floors were white, turn-of-the-century bathroom tiles. Old beer posters decorated the oak walls—not the faux posters decorators were putting up in single's saloons uptown. This was the real thing. But it was a dim, colorless place; a place full of promises, envies, and regret.

Rory, the bartender, moved from one end of the bar to another, flipping taps, splashing glasses, sliding a cloth across the shiny wood, then placing coasters in front of his customers. Alan noticed the illuminated containers of green limes, lemon peels, and maraschino cherries beside the vodka bottles.

"Hey Alan, sorry I'm late."

Bill took off his suit coat, draped it over the back of the wooden bar chair, and sat down.

"Glad you could make it. As you can see, I couldn't wait to order. What'll you have?"

"Scotch on the rocks." Rory overheard and nodded.

"I can't believe all this, Alan. It blew my mind when I heard."

"You and me both, chum."

"What can you tell me? You know I'll do what I can."

Rory placed an old-fashioned glass on a cardboard coaster and centered it in front of Bill.

Time had flown unnaturally fast over the week or so since Alan had marched into the president's office with his secret about the Wholesome Soup account. He had fled in confusion to the country that evening, wondering all weekend why Wally Hendricks might be returning to Dunaway months after taking a creative job at Baker and Dodge. But then all was made clear on Monday afternoon in the account management conference room. Alan had realized that the events underway resulted from backroom deal-making beyond anything he had imagined. This was not the advertising business of his early days when an agency was named for the men at the top. Or was it?

Alan described the series of events to Bill; how at the Monday meeting Bob Howe had introduced the new creative leadership: Tom Hartley would head the creative department and Wally would lead a new group—including a few people brought over from Baker. Lou was out; he hadn't come to the office that day. Alan had huddled with his group the rest of the afternoon—doing his best to keep them from criticizing the agency's decision. He told them to wait and see, keep their heads, while the whole time his head had wanted to explode. Alan himself had been left with a choice: lose his place, his relevance in the agency, or leave. All week he had worked on his resume.

Alan ordered another cold beer and a second scotch for Bill. "It is just business, Alan," Bill said, attempting to commiserate. Alan knew Bill meant well, but he couldn't absorb Bill's words. He switched the topic.

"So, how's the old lady, Bill?"

"A little pissed off right now, Alan."

Bill's family went to Stockbridge, Massachusetts, in the summer. From Memorial Day to mid-September he wandered around a nine-room apartment in the enormous, block-long building on 94th Street and Park Avenue whose entrance was a sweeping courtyard with a full circle drive for taxis and private cars.

During the year, the Taylors frequently entertained; their apartment perfectly decorated à la *Town & Country*. (Bill's wife's father was a millionaire who belonged to the New York Yacht Club.) Yet for three and a half months in the summer the apartment became a bachelor officer's quarters, with one bachelor officer, one maid, and a cook.

"Frankly, I'd have preferred your hassle to the one I'm in now," Bill said, looking at his drink.

"Oh no, this sounds bad."

"Yeah, I came back from a business trip in Europe and like an ass went straight through from Boston to Stockbridge."

"What's wrong with that? Christ, it beats going through JFK and all the hassle of driving upstate."

"Anyway, Angela is royally pissed."

"All because you flew direct through Boston?"

"It's not that. I had my bag with me with all my dirty clothes. She opened it to sort out the things to be laundered and dry-cleaned."

"You left something in the bag you shouldn't have?" Alan put his mug back on the coaster. One swallow. Half a mug.

"Worse. A pair of pajamas." Bill was shaking his head, staring empty-eyed out the door onto 1st Avenue.

"Uh-oh, something on the pajamas?" This felt like twenty questions.

Bill nodded without looking at Alan.

"Why in God's name do you still wear pajamas?" Alan cringed at himself for saying this aloud. "Sorry, go on."

"I always do when I travel abroad." Bill often sounded like William F. Buckley, Alan thought.

"So, what's the story? The pajamas smell of perfume? You spill something on them? What?"

"Lipstick, Alan."

"Oh my God, not..." Alan started to chuckle while Bill explained in detail.

"Alan, this isn't a funny matter! I mean, Angela is all set to hang those clothes from the terrace with a note saying 'get in touch with my lawyer.'"

"Jesus, man. But that's ridiculous. You were in Europe, not 42nd Street! You were probably hammered in your Paris hotel with some gal. You probably don't remember it anyway."

"Unfortunately, I remember it vividly." His brow arched.

"Well, I don't mean to pry, but has Angela never done it like that?"

"Never."

Alan was surprised at this. Angela Taylor had a cat-like quality Alan found interesting. He imagined she would have had some very unusual moves.

"I have tried a lot of those sexology things; I tried getting her to read that one by the man and woman doctors."

"I don't think they're medical doctors, are they?"

"I'm serious, Alan, Angela is furious and hurt. I don't know what the hell to do."

"Only one thing to do, Bill. Show her you love her. Take her some-place. Take time off if you have to. Listen to her, then show her you love her."

Alan smiled and picked up his mug of beer and finished it. Rory, sensing it was time for round three, was hovering nearby and quickly moved in to take their glasses.

"That's it, Rory, my friend. Just the check. Got to find our way to the uptown subway."

They paid the bill.

"You know what to do man. You just said it," Alan continued. He tried not to sound too much like a newspaper column. "Tell her you're sorry, but be straight with her. Tell her that, as a grown-up man with a lot of basic instincts and drives and curiosity, you think there's more to sex than what you just said. The lying on top bit."

"You think it's that simple."

"It's all you got going for you so far."

"Well," Bill said in his best Groton accent, "I'll give it a go."

They picked up their blazers and shook hands.

"Call me if you are serious about looking at other agencies, Alan. I'll write you a letter about the awards. I know you don't need it—you have miles of credits—but I am happy to help."

"Thanks, buddy. I hope I didn't keep you out too late. Call her and tell her you are coming to Stockbridge tomorrow night."

Alan turned from his friend to walk the few blocks to the subway. The beer and the talking hadn't helped him the way he had hoped. Bill's story had only heightened his own dread: he also had a phone call to make. What would he say to Liddie? Bill at least had Angela. Would Liddie ever understand?

20

Alan slid the pay phone door shut while he waited for Wally to come on the line. The booth was sweltering.

"Walter, how are you? Can we still meet this afternoon?"

"Hiya Alan. Sure, come on by." Wally sounded slightly out of breath.

"Do you have any beer on hand?"

"No, you'd better stop and get some. I can't keep beer in this goddamn place for more than an hour."

"Are you mobbed right now?"

"No, but I'm doing a dirty puzzle. So, hurry up. It's getting to the good parts."

Wally hung up. The guy had no class.

Alan stopped off at a small delicatessen on 54th Street and walked out with a six-pack of Michelob. The day was hot, clammy, and gray. Alan noted the shorter skirts on the girls crossing Park Avenue.

He had been told to check in with the guard before going up to his old offices at Dunaway to meet with Wally. He managed to catch Mr. Harris's eye and nodded a greeting. The guard lifted his hand, acknowledging Alan as if it were a normal day. Alan didn't feel betrayed as he had expected, nor resentful, nor suspicious. Strangely, he didn't feel anything. A glass mirror on the wall invited him to look at himself. Light gray suit, white shirt, red tie. Not bad, he thought. It must have been the lighting, the suit looked new. His own face appeared surprisingly rested and composed, certainly not the way he felt. Had he slept well?

Was it his imagination, or were the brass plates around the elevator buttons unpolished? The textured wallpaper peeling where it met the once-glossy black floor? The elevator opened. Two well-dressed men got out, laughing.

"On the waterbed!" one exclaimed.

"And you fixed them up?" the other squeaked as they passed.

The elevator smelled heavily of aftershave.

In the northwest corner of the thirty-fourth floor a young secretary in lime green with Lynn Redgrave hair smiled at Alan and gestured for him to go in.

The door to Wally's new corner office was ajar, and Alan could hear music from inside. What a way to work, he thought.

"Hello sport." Wally grinned and got up to shake Alan's hand. Despite the recent mess, he seemed to think they were old and good pals still.

It seemed like only a few weeks had passed, but already Wally had transformed Lou's office into a living room: stainless steel drooping floor lamps, two oversized and overstuffed sofas facing each other, a glass-topped table with three different pastel-colored phones on it, copies of *Motion Picture Daily* and *Variety*. He had been sitting at a black, half-moon shaped desk.

The yellow phone rang, and Wally walked over and picked it up. Alan could hear the secretary's voice through the open door.

"Mr. Hendricks, it's Mel Fox from Filmgems on two."

Wally pressed the two button. Alan turned and sat gingerly on one of the sofas.

"Let's say Wednesday. Mickey's? God, not that toilet!"

Alan took a deep breath.

Wally loudly hung up the phone.

"So, Alan. Here we are," he declared, returning to his desk chair.

"No, Wally, you are here. I'm out."

"You could have stayed; I told you it would be new. And Tom assured us both that you have a place if you want it. It's the work that has to change, Alan. Jamesville is no different than the rest; they want impact, emotion."

"Cut the crap, Wally. What I want to know is how you did it. How did you get to Bob Howe? He's a meat and potatoes sort of guy. He doesn't have an imagination. How did you get to him?"

Wally turned his designer office chair playfully from side to side.

"Well, I guess you could say I double-crossed Baker."

"They were pretty sure they had the business. I talked to an old friend…"

"Exactly. Baker and Dodge presented a campaign that had only about one less platitude than the Dunaway boards." Wally looked at his nails.

"Thanks a lot."

"It was good work; the suburban farm scenes reminded me of *Mister Ed*—funny show. But Alan, they cancelled *Mister Ed* over a year ago. The thing is, Charlie Whacker at Baker didn't know that I had friends at Jamesville."

"No shit."

"Remember Mike, the red-headed fellow at the presentation? He's actually the son of Old Man Jamesville, and I went to college with him. Well, really, I went to the student bar with him and we shared a girlfriend at one point, but he's hip. And he's VP. He wants creative, animated advertising. Believes that a new campaign will prove his value to his father and the company.

"So, I show Bob Howe the boards I worked up that I know Mike likes, and I tell Bob that if he brings me back as creative supervisor, Dunaway has Jamesville."

All the meetings and phone calls, the work, the dozens of boards that the art directors had drawn and tossed—all at Alan's bidding. The lost weekend, the call from Buffy—scenes swirled around in his head, and for a minute Alan thought he heard voices.

One of the pastel-colored phones on the table began to ring. Alan looked at the table: yellow, blue, and pink. How would Wally know which one to pick up?

* * *

Something shoved him.

"Alan, wake up! That's the next gal."

Alan opened his eyes. Mel Fox leaned over him, his bronze neck setting off a thick, gold chain.

"Alan, man! You dozed off. The last model is here for the older gal part. We need to get through so we can go to lunch. Everyone is starved. You okay?"

Alan shook his head. Hollywood! The casting session.

"But we already chose. Didn't we? You said I'd like her. Claire Whitman. Just now."

"What? No, Alan, you must have been really out of it. It's the next gal, Jill, I thought you'd like. And here she is!" Mel was walking to the door.

"Wow." Alan stood to shake her hand. Must be those beds at the Beverly Hills Hotel.

21

Alan flew home overnight from the coast. The surly cab driver who had picked him up at Kennedy Airport made a U-turn to drop him at his building.

It was still dark. An unfamiliar overnight doorman stood sleepily to let him in. Alan dropped his bags in the lobby and wrenched the mail out of the overstuffed box. Such a simple thing, one's own mail. A couple of slick adverts slipped onto the floor, but he was glad to pick them up. He was on the ground, in his own building. He'd made it home.

When he got up to the apartment he changed to khakis and then went through the bills and letters in the front hall. Before he slept, he needed breakfast, and he craved some orange juice. He had become accustomed to the fresh orange juice served each morning at the Beverly Hills Hotel. The bottled juice at the market would be inferior, but he grabbed his wallet anyway and headed down the elevator and back outside to walk the three blocks to the market.

The sun was up but low behind the buildings. An occasional taxi heading down Park Avenue hardly disturbed the neighborhood's repose. He passed one guy arranging suitcases in the trunk of a double-parked car and an elderly lady waiting for her feeble gray poodle to go.

He felt hungover, either from the flight or from spending a whole week in Lotus Land, as they called it, or from the drinks—probably not a good idea—that he'd had on the plane to help himself sleep. It was Friday. He had the day to recuperate, and then he would take the train to the country.

He crossed Lexington at the red "Don't Walk" sign, no traffic in sight. He loved doing that. The city felt like a different place at this hour, a place he wasn't normally permitted to see, like walking into an empty theater between shows. The unfamiliar long shadows and the shouts of sunlight here and there altered what seemed unalterable: the dingy commercial block below 3rd Avenue looked less grim, less neglected. Or maybe the blue sky somehow upstaged the filthy signs, torn awnings, and rusted gates.

Maybe he was just glad to see a little dirt after the shiny perfection of the West Coast.

Was the market open at this hour on a Friday? He tried the door, and to his relief it gave way and, he slid inside where it was cool and smelled like carrot greens, bologna, damp saw dust, and old coffee grounds.

With a small bundle he walked back to the apartment. Provisions: bread, milk, marg, OJ, green apples, a potato, and a steak. The outing made him feel renewed, replanted.

His mind returned to the matters he had been contemplating on the plane east (with the aid of gin and Schweppes tonic water).

He had had a disturbing dream that first day in Hollywood. Not like him to nod off at a casting session, but no one said much about it, and he made up for his lapse twice over in managing an excellent shoot: good talent, a no-bullshit director, and Mel, who, however annoying, went along with his decisions and managed to charm the studio people to do the same.

As he recalled the details of the trip, feelings of self-doubt and uncertainty began to grow, and he had to will his mind to relax, to take in the quiet of the walk back to his apartment building. But with each step his thoughts snuck back to that first morning when he had fallen asleep. He had tried to forget that dream, but on the plane he couldn't help himself—he had revisited some parts of it again and again.

The dream had seemed so real, like he had seen the future, or experienced a parallel life. Wasn't that a theory of Einstein's? Where had he heard that? It embarrassed him to think this way; pop psychology was not his thing.

He remembered he had feverishly been trying to save an advertising campaign, all the while being tricked. The whole thing was a ruse, like he was a rat in a cage madly stepping on a lever, on and on, not knowing that the reward will never come. The effort he had made in the dream was all for nothing, and worse, he had been duped somehow. Wally, his friend, had betrayed him. Wally a turncoat with himself ending up expendable, tossed aside, inconsequential.

Had it been his fault somehow? He couldn't remember, but he also couldn't figure out the lesson; there had to be a lesson. Weren't dreams supposed to have lessons? His efforts had been pointless, was it all pointless? That's what he had begun to wonder. The whole advertising business, the business he worked on every day. What was the point of it? For him, for Alan.

He did used to love it, ad-making, but not so much anymore, not the business of advertising. Christ, stop making such a big deal, he thought. I like my job! I'm just worn out from the phony Hollywood bullshit.

Claire Whitman had been in the dream too. At one point she had impossibly walked in the door of Mel's casting session. Then they were by the hotel pool, and she (all wet and so sexy, her indifference to him declaring his inadequacy) dared him to push himself, to take a risk. Was it something specific? He couldn't recall, but something big—that's what it seemed like. Had he lost his edge? Is that what she'd said?

Maybe he should change jobs—hell, maybe change careers! That had occurred to him on the plane. A frightening idea. Was that what the dream was telling him?

He had sat on the plane and made lists of what he loved and hated about the job at Dunaway, of agencies and client companies he knew or would ever consider working for. A dream made him do all that! Ridiculous. But he had felt better afterward.

Claire had certainly done a number on him. In the dream, it was as if she knew him from years ago and saw through him now. He had felt a little bit that way on their innocent date two weeks before the business trip. She had intrigued him with her freedom, her edge, and her smarts. Their easy wordplay—how they clicked—had actually scared him a little. Of course, she also made his intestines go into knots—he flushed ten degrees hotter at the thought of her even now, or maybe it was the sun on his back walking up this hill.

Standing in the elevator, it struck him that Liddie had not appeared in the dream, had seemed to have no place. That was big. Bigger than anything else.

As he turned the key to their apartment, he knew he would have to face that someday—his marriage—but he wasn't ready yet; it was still only the first week of August.

* * *

Alan returned to work the following Monday.

Tom Hartley stopped into Alan's office that morning ostensibly to talk about the previous week, but, like it always did, the conversation devolved. What struck Alan the most was that he didn't find any of it funny. Tom Hartley was the leader of the pack when it came to summer "diversions," but his latest tales had given Alan a feeling of unease that he hadn't felt before.

Tom had leaned in Alan's door around nine wearing a striped shirt open at the neck, sleeves rolled up, no tie, and his wavy black hair curled around his ears.

"Busy?"

"Of course not, just back from a week away! Have a seat. I have a half hour—are you coming to the Lucky Stores meeting today?" Alan asked.

"Nope," Tom replied. He had taken the wide leather chair by the window. "I gave the art director what he needed on Friday. But I thought you might want details of what happened around here last week so you would impress everybody—like the master you are."

"Thanks," Alan said with a two-fingered gesture like a salute. "I appreciate everything. I hear the new account man on this seems to have trouble with original ideas. He has been a pain in the ass."

Tom snickered. He and Alan both knew the drill. Account people always questioned the creative department. But account men were forced to live by contracts and deadlines.

"How'd it go out there?" Tom asked. "Get any action on the casting couch?"

Alan smiled but felt a jab of embarrassment. "We have footage for at least three good, thirty-second commercials," he said, "and much as Mel tried, I didn't take the bait. No girls, no dates."

Tom shook his head and sighed with disappointment.

They talked about the dynamics of working with Mel. Alan described the near disaster in one California store when, setting up for a shoot, the film crew blew the electrical circuits, shutting down the meat department refrigerators. They laughed.

"All in a day's work!" Tom quipped.

Alan picked up the phone to ask Doris for some coffee.

"You like cream, right?" He asked, looking back at Tom. As they continued, Doris appeared with two mugs, her roundness held together in a snug gray dress with too many buttons.

"Thanks, Doris. How are the session arrangements going, Tom?" Alan asked. Doris turned and left.

Tom complained about scheduling the studio musicians. There had also been an art department meltdown that he had resolved and a disagreement over some graphics.

"They still might be late," he explained. "But it all turned out great, and you are on track. So, now can I tell you the real reason I came in here?"

"Go on, but make it quick."

"I took up with a girl who writes copy for *CBS News*."

"Oh, not another!" Alan listened with one ear. What do they see in him? he thought. He's a smooth talker, but he's noisy and petulant. He's loyal to his friends, but a complete con man. Maybe it's the hair: girls find that sexy. And what about Ella? He's a lucky man to have a wife like her.

"This one is twenty-five, and she has a Labrador retriever," Tom continued. "She wants to bring the dog to my apartment."

Alan played along.

"Where does he sleep at her place?"

"At the foot of the bed. I thought one night, the way he jumped on the bed, that the son of a bitch would break my ankles."

Alan began to feel annoyed. Tom was leaning back, the view of rooftops and water towers stretching far beyond him out the window. Was he for real? Yes, Alan thought. Remember the last story about the newscaster? But that had been funny, hadn't it?

Tom was still talking.

"And the hamburger bills were unbelievable."

"You bought hamburger? What, to win him over?"

"Yeah, to show I was pet-friendly."

"You know a dog can die from hamburger meat," Alan replied cautiously as he licked the sugar from the teaspoon in his cup. "In fact, a dog could die on sirloin if that's all you fed him. I read that in some research briefs."

"Well, he doesn't get sirloin. And he doesn't get top round either. Just hamburger. And it's bloody expensive."

Was Tom boasting? Alan thought.

"Does he like you?" Alan asked.

"Not particularly. But he isn't an angry dog or anything. Not like a police dog or a Scottie."

"Scottie?"

"Mean bastards. Really mean."

They both laughed at the absurdity. Tom obviously enjoyed sharing his yarns, and he was laughing at himself, but there was something pathetic about the whole thing, and Alan felt Tom knew it too.

"Time for me to get to that meeting," Alan said, turning to his desk.

"Sure. Fill me in later," Tom said, stealing a coke from Alan's fridge as he moved toward the door.

"And for what it's worth, drop the dog."

"Yeah. Thanks." Tom strode away up the hall past Doris's desk.

Alan rose, chose a sharp pencil from his pencil cup, and grabbed a blank pad. Was this boredom or disgust he felt?

The whole thing wasn't funny. Like a Red Skelton gag he'd seen too many times. Had he lost his sense of humor? First day back at work and something had definitely changed.

22

"If I were running the account management of this fucking agency, I'd get Dick Fields out of here," Charlie Ogden, Alan's art director, said as he whipsawed a metal ruler on his drawing board.

Alan continued doodling in the border of an agency memo. He was supposed to be reading a set of contact reports—lists of meetings and phone calls with agency clients—for TransUS Airlines, the client that was looking to promote new routes.

"He's an ass," Buck Jones muttered, standing beside Charlie, looking at the boards. He chewed the end of a pencil like he was waiting to tell Charlie his next idea for the layout. The three men had occupied Charlie's corner of the art department. Their meeting had bled over into the lunch hour.

"Well, I am not sure I would put it that way," Alan responded. "But the man seems to know only one way—one style—and now he's on all new business, including this. I don't understand it either."

Alan had hired Buck as a copywriter for the TransUS Airlines account earlier in the summer. Hiring Buck was the centerpiece of his strategy to try and get TransUS international routes for Dunaway. Then, upon arriving back from California, Alan's excitement had been dashed. Bob Wilson, the malleable and good-natured account supervisor, was nowhere to be found. The agency president had made Fields de facto 'prime minister' by appointing him to run the new business operation. Fields was a longtime research man whose one and only account management credit was a big cereal company.

All Alan could do was maneuver to get the airline's business while not pissing off Fields. TransUS had changed agencies twice in an effort to jazz up marketing its domestic flights. They had turned heads hiring Pando McCabe to sell their coast-to-coast routes. In all, Alan understood that they had worked with three good agencies, so the competition for this new brand assignment would be tough.

"Landon says he's like a Sherman tank. No finesse. No wit. No class," Buck commented, referring to their frequent lunch buddy in the accounts department.

"He's certainly wrong for this," Alan said, looking increasingly frustrated as he tried to decipher the notes on the contact reports.

"I guess there is nothing to do about it until he makes enough mistakes. They say Fields has been here for twenty years," said Charlie, who had put down his pencil and was looking at Alan from behind his glasses and that awful fringe of brown hair.

"Yeah, but I have to give the TransUS new business presentation with him next week. We can't let him screw this up. Chatting with him yesterday, it was pretty clear he has no sense of how to appeal to the company representatives, two of whom, by the way, are pilots turned businessmen."

Was the air conditioning off? Alan felt himself perspire as he imagined sitting there with Fields at the end of the long conference room table as the company reps grimly closed their briefcases to go.

"What are you going to do?" Buck asked.

"Show them the reel. Show them some print. A few case histories." Alan tried not to sound resigned.

"God, that sounds dreary," Charlie said, looking back at his drawing board.

"That's what Fields wants to do."

"Nobody cares about case histories," Buck exclaimed. "Let me do the presentation, Alan. Shit, let me do the talkin', and I'll show them there's money in those pretty storyboards Charlie here has made for us." Buck was walking back and forth as he spoke. He rolled up his sleeves. His leather boots squeaked.

"You know, that's not a bad idea," Alan said. He leaned back and looked at Charlie with a smile. "Put a good-looking cowboy in a meeting with a couple of former fighter pilots."

"Hey, I like bullshitting with guys who like to go fast!" Buck was smiling now.

"All we'd need is a campfire," Charlie added.

"Seriously men, I think you have something here."

Alan had a plan.

* * *

The next day Alan was at his desk at nine, looking through an agency proof book—pages of color and black-and-white advertisements J Dunaway Advertising had produced, including many from his own group. He was astonished at how little marketing to business customers the agency did.

And we're pitching an airlines account, he thought.

"Anybody home?" Dick Fields stuck his enormous head inside Alan's doorway, a cigar the size of a piece of pipe stuck in his mouth. Unlit, thankfully.

"Sure, Dick. Come on in."

"How are we doing on the TransUS Airlines presentation?"

"Just fine."

"I am hoping we can focus on print advertising."

"Among other things, sure. But why the special concern?"

"That's primarily what the client is after. I thought I mentioned it."

Although Buck and the copywriters in his group had good ideas that would work in print, they had been thinking television. Dick knew the basic pitch of the advertising but nothing more. Alan had been avoiding him to give his group some creative space.

Dick was now the number-two man at the agency, a political appointee. Alan knew he had to slow his approach to this conversation. Bank right and pull back on the throttle. No sarcasm.

"Let's think about that, Dick. I happen to have the agency proofs right here. We don't do much print at Dunaway." Don't be a smart-ass, he cautioned himself.

"Don't we have any Intercontinental Metals proofs we could show them?"

"We don't have that account anymore, Dick. That was five years ago."

"When did that make any difference? We did the work, didn't we?"

"Dick, the agency is eighty-five percent television now, but I'll find some print. Please. Let me handle the creative part of this."

Why was Fields so fixated on print? Must be feeling out of his league.

"Well, do it your way, but I know Steve is going to be looking to see what we can do in print."

"Who is Steve?"

"The ad manager for TransUS."

"So, he makes the decision?"

"That's my guess."

What an answer, Alan thought. An account manager should know the informal client hierarchy. His heart thumped in his chest. He realized he was holding his breath.

"I need to get back to work, Dick."

"We'll have a run-through, of course." The statement was half-question and half-order.

"What's to run through? We've done this before. You know how I present. You've heard the idea."

Of course, Alan's plan was to have Buck Jones present; the two of them had planned it out the day before. Alan would introduce the presentation, teasing the client's sensibilities, and then Buck would take over, showing the boards—a strong contrast in voice and outlook, Buck's all-American to Alan's refined New York executive.

Alan was sure TransUS was looking for something bold and adventurous for advertising their overseas routes to business customers.

Dunaway would give them more than that. But Dick would never go for Buck Jones giving the pitch. He might block them if he knew of the plan. Would a phony run-through work? If they had to, they would surprise him, flatter him throughout, and by the end, when the two pilots were nodding their heads, Dick would insist it was all him.

"This is a different kind of account," Fields replied.

"You bet it is and we have it wrapped up. When's the meeting?"

"Next week, Wednesday at twelve."

"Where?"

"My office." Fields finally lit the foot-long cigar. The first puff rolled toward Alan's desk. Right at him.

"Your office is a little formal, don't you think?" Alan asked with restraint. Dick Field's office was one big Currier and Ives horse print.

"Well, we can have lunch in there and then go to the creative conference room for your part."

"Why don't we do the creative part first, in the screening room, then have lunch?"

"Because that's not the way I want to do it."

"Will anyone else be there from account management?"

"I'll see you then." Fields stepped out the door, ignoring the question.

* * *

Alan turned to face the window. He watched a tug pulling a barge filled with rubbish down the East River. Yesterday he had felt momentarily inspired by Buck's enthusiasm. He too had wanted to show this major airline client what he was worth—he had wanted to take a risk for a change! Now he felt a gray uncertainty descend. Maybe I should do this one by the book, he thought now. Do what Fields wants, present the reel, show some print, tell a few case histories. Why did he feel so invested? Alan felt helpless. They wouldn't get the business, not with this guy.

23

The cab was stuck on 51th Street. They crawled along across town behind a line of small trucks making deliveries and impatient yellow cabs. Alan and Tom had decided to share the fare down to Grand Central after their Thursday afternoon meeting at 53rd and 5th, and both regretted it now.

"Summer is over," Tom said, staring out the open window. He watched a weary man pushing a hand truck piled with crushed vegetable boxes and a laborer resting on his shovel, smoking.

"What do you mean, Tom? It isn't even Labor Day." Alan felt the slight breeze as the cab approached the corner. Traffic was flying uptown on Madison.

"Summer is over. I'm tired of chasing around. Nothing's happened anyway, no luck meeting the girl of my dreams. Not this summer. What does that bullshit mean anyway? I'm going home for a long weekend to get to know the real Mrs. Hartley again."

Alan wondered if he was witnessing another one of Tom's occasional slips into 'self-exploration.' Tom had read a bunch of psychology books, and Alan presumed he used most of what he learned from them for his come-ons.

Tom was a tom. Like a stray cat every summer. Alan could count on him for enlightenment on sexual matters beyond his own expertise, or in other words, a good dirty story. Of all people, Tom was not one who seemed to need any 'masculine validation.' So, Alan was struck now to hear him voice self-doubt.

"That bad?"

"Yes, it was. It started out promising enough, but I realized a few things. In June, I met a crazy production house rep who knew lots of models. He had a great pad. Lots of floor cushions. Served hot dogs and sauerkraut for dinner…"

"That sounds classy." Alan felt like he was in a one of those PSAs for young people that warns them about peer pressure.

Tom ignored Alan's sarcasm.

"They'd pass a joint around—which I always passed up—I don't like to drink and smoke that stuff. Anyway, I went to his place a few times. Took the train out there. Met some young ladies, girls really. They were nineteen and twenty, pretty enough. But I really felt the age spread."

Alan felt a drip of perspiration run down his neck. Hadn't he felt the same way? The insipid chatter of the girls he'd met through Wally last year. The boredom of not caring. He turned his head to hear Tom over the sirens and the jackhammers, watching Tom's flushed face, his eyes focused on the scene out the windshield and on the movement of people and garbage out the open side window. Alan's head ached with the exhaust fumes, the heat, and his own thoughts. Tom's confession had hit a nerve.

"I get you, man," Alan said, meaning it.

"…and there wasn't anything to talk about. I had to lead every conversation. Without fail, it began with me asking, Where are you from? San Francisco. What part? Well, not in the city exactly. Oh, Sausalito? No. The peninsula? No, Oakland. Oh. I can't wait to get back to California… It was pretty much like that every time."

Alan took a Chicklet from his breast pocket. Tom continued.

"There was the gal with the dog. I told you about her. And then last week I had a blind date. Met her at the Berkshire. Took her to Martell's for a cheeseburger. A stinger at Elaine's. Back to the chick's pad and then—you'll love this—the roommate was still up! It felt too uncomfortable. So, I split. Walked all the way home."

Tom turned to Alan and looked him in the eye.

"I called the girl the next day and made my excuses."

"Always the gentleman."

"No joke, Alan! It's just not worth it."

Alan looked ahead as the cab surged forward and around the corner onto Amsterdam Avenue. The cab pulled to the curb.

Alan had his wallet out first. "I got this," he said. He waved Tom out of the cab and handed the cabbie his fare.

"Keep the change, sir."

In the Great Hall, Tom looked for the gate announcement for the Long Island Railroad while Alan scanned the board for the *Merchants Limited.*

They shook hands. One in their disconsolation.

"So, like I say Alan, the summer is over."

"As they say in your books, 'I hear what you are saying' and, while I don't like to admit defeat, I too am done."

* * *

The following Sunday afternoon, a tall, tanned young man in his early thirties, carrying a soft leather Abercrombie & Fitch weekender with a squash racquet sticking out, walked up to Alan Robinson at the New London station.

"Which end is the parlor car tonight, Alan?"

Alan had been staring at a white-hulled yawl reaching up the Thames River toward the two bridges that crossed the river between New London and Groton, Connecticut. Smaller boats sped up and down the river. Across the water, the quick blinding lights of acetylene torches winked from within the enormous green shed of Electric Boat Company. Inside, a nuclear submarine was being welded together.

"They didn't announce it. But it's been forward since Memorial Day weekend."

"You never know with these bastards."

The young man carrying the squash racquet was one of the Fishers Island summer residents who caught the last ferry Sunday nights. There were usually fifteen or twenty from Fishers who took the train, all shaved and suited in linen or seersucker or lightweight J. Press synthetic weaves. Madras ties and Gucci loafers. Except for Dave Chase, he couldn't believe that the Fishers Island people had anything going on in New York when they got to town. He was convinced their dressing-up was habit.

Alan looked like he always did these days on Sunday evenings going to New York. He wore a pair of khakis with a faded Lacoste shirt and loafers—he prided himself on having the only pair of loafers on the train without the little brass thing on the top—without socks. Alan never dressed for the trip to New York. There was no reason to wreck a shirt and un-press a pair of trousers; he hadn't shaved since Saturday morning.

The first time he took the Sunday-night parlor car to the city, as he started to board the porter had looked him over and then said deferentially, "This is Parlor Car 1743, sir."

Alan had smiled at the porter's diplomacy and said, "Thank you, I know. I have a chair reserved for the summer. Every Sunday night on the 6:49."

"I see, sir. Yes, sir."

That was three years ago, and the Sunday night routine remained the same. Same people from Fishers. Same people from Pequot. Same people from Old Black Point and back country.

"Say, Alan, which end of the train's the parlor car on tonight?" It was Peyton Patterson, another Fishers Islander, same age as Alan, a Wall Street investment banker.

"Beats me, Peyton. They haven't announced it. But like I told Tad here, it's been up front since Memorial Day weekend."

Why do they ask me? Alan thought.

The three made small talk about the weekend.

"There it is," somebody said, pointing to the thin black string of passenger cars crossing the railroad bridge up the river. The hum of the engines and the distant clack-clack of the cars on the bridge were familiar sounds to most on the platform. Hearing the approaching train, each person reached mechanically for a briefcase or valise. The parlor car ticket-holders slowly moved forward; the coach passengers who were regulars listlessly started back toward the mail carts; and the rest, not knowing the ritual, stood uncertainly in the middle, wondering why the crowd was dispersing.

The train's brakes spat out sparks; the roar between the train and the station as loud as any subway train. Alan walked with the rest of the parlor car passengers to the first car behind the hissing, diesel locomotive. A tall Black porter in a mustard colored uniform was wiping the handrails at the doorway leading onto the parlor car.

"Evening, Mister Lumpkin." Alan nodded and smiled at the porter.

"Evening, sir."

"Hi, Lump," bellowed one of the Fishers Islanders as he hopped up onto the parlor car steps. Each passenger in his turn greeted the porter. It was that informal and that regular.

As always, Alan claimed a seat in the middle of the car overlooking the seaside. He put his bag overhead and sat. He knew every turn on the coastal trip. Before Old Saybrook, he enjoyed watching the bathers and the couples huddled together on blankets along the Niantic public beach wave to the train as it roared past.

Lucky, Alan thought.

"Share a ride uptown, Alan?" The voice belonged to Peter Wells, the fellow Pequot Islander. Peter was an advertising salesman with *Time, Inc.* He stood, bags in hand, beside Alan's seat.

"Sure."

Alan noted that Wells was dressed in his usual tasseled loafers and snap brim straw hat with a madras hatband.

"Anybody else going uptown?"

"Usually Dave Chase goes up with me to his place on 93rd and Park, but I don't see him." Alan paused, then added, "Peter, why do you get all dressed for this train ride back to the city?"

Wells smiled. "Ever been to Rum's on Sunday night, Alan?"

"Never even heard of it."

"Well, I'll tell you. Drop in some Sunday night after you get to New York, and I guarantee you'll shave and start wearing something a little better-looking than that outfit."

"What is it? A pick up joint?" asked Alan.

"Not exactly. Some music and a lot of airline stews and gals in from Fire Island. Good spot. A lot of guys go there."

"I'm too tired for that stuff, Peter. This train ride alone is a crusher. I'd rather have a bottle of Majorska and watch reruns of *Bachelor Father*."

As soon as he said it, he wondered at himself. He had had his own excitement in the city earlier in the summer, but the romance with Lina, his stunning model, was over, and the trip to the coast had knocked the air out of him.

Wells smiled like a wily high schooler.

"Well, once you're a summer bachelor a little longer, I think you'll see it a little differently." He moved ahead to find a seat.

Alan turned and looked out at the pink caste of Long Island Sound. Summer bachelor, he thought, sighing. This weekend, for first time in months, he had truly enjoyed being in the country with the boys and Liddie. Something had changed in him, a darkness had lifted, and he saw the bigger picture, the stacked deck.

That was it. He had been managing this play-within-a-play for far too long. Since Lina, and then meeting Claire, he had been constantly thinking of the inevitable conversation with Liddie that would lay waste to fourteen years of marriage. How would it start? Where would they be? Keeping up this routine, wearing his frayed shirt, gave him some relief from his dread. It was just a matter of time.

Or was it? Did everything with Liddie need to go up in smoke? What about Dunaway and all the corporate bullshit? Was there a way out?

He wondered about Claire. She had left him a message at the office on Friday. She really was in California on business. The job with the record label had come through, and she would be based in New York. For a moment he imagined her in the purple suit she had worn when he met her at Dunaway. He wanted to see her again, but not for the usual reasons.

The train slowed as it approached the Connecticut River Bridge. The sun dipped behind the low, uneven line of pine trees to the west of the river as the train made the wide, slow turn onto the iron bridge. Four sailboats, waiting to complete the trip upriver to Hamburg Cove, rocked gently in the outgoing tide below the bridge.

Alan found pleasure in this part of the trip. The wetlands on the west side of the river were nesting places for swans and terns. On top of a telephone pole, the oversized, scraggly nest of an osprey sat silhouetted against the distant, blue-gray finger of land that disappeared into Long Island Sound at the mouth of the river. Pretty, he thought.

"So, I'll meet you by the taxi stand," Peter Wells's voice cut though Alan's thoughts, interrupting the soft clack of the train as it slowly crossed the bridge. Peter stood in the aisle, holding the chair backs to steady himself.

"But Peter, why bother to go uptown if you're going to this Rum's place?"

"Gotta leave off the briefcase."

"Christ, I'll drop it off with the doorman!"

"No. It's ritual, Alan. I've been doing it for years. No sense inviting the guy's curiosity."

What was he doing conspiring with this tanned millionaire's son in his phony straw hat? This guy is despicable, Alan thought. All of a sudden, the semblance of order he had pieced together over the weekend began to come apart. He was heading right into it again.

What had Tom said on Friday? "It's not worth it."

"Actually Peter, I can't, uh, share a cab. I need to get straight to the apartment tonight." Alan pulled his briefcase onto his lap and snapped open the locks. He overcame a momentary instinct to disappear into the corners and pockets, his private hallways and rooms where he could be alone with his thoughts.

"But good luck, tonight," Alan said, looking up coolly.

"Okay, then," muttered Peter, his glee snuffed out. He retreated to his seat a few rows away just as the engineer blew two blasts for the crossings at Guilford.

24

Claire looked at the watch on the inside of her wrist. The waiter hovered over the two women at the table next to hers, pointing to the menu with his pen, waving his pen in the air, resting it on his stubbly chin. He seemed to charm the younger woman, but her companion looked from the menu to the waiter with suspicion and distaste, as if she had stopped for directions in a bad part of town.

Alan was late. Maybe he had stood her up. She hadn't confirmed their meeting. Joyce, Claire's new secretary, said she had called his number and left a message with his secretary. A Midtown lunch had seemed harmless enough. She liked him, but she wanted to make it clear: he was married. She had no interest in being another conquest, and she was sure he was that type. But she liked him, the banter, the shoptalk, and sure, the flirtation. Well, hardly shoptalk—she didn't know much about ad agencies—but work talk. He had experience in things she wanted to know more about, so she wanted to continue the relationship, meet for lunch, like people did. She knew she had to be careful, to nip things in the bud if he had any fantasies of romance. It had felt slightly that way on the ferry ride in July, and she suspected that if she had to say anything directly today, he'd probably not meet for any future lunches.

She turned her thoughts to her afternoon. She had a one thirty meeting with a studio executive. She plotted the distance to the meeting and the time she needed, factoring in the elevator wait, her sore heels, and crossing Park Avenue in one hundred percent humidity.

She'd meet Herman, her boss, there. He would lead this first meeting, he had said, then she'd take over next week. He was giving

Claire complete control of marketing a female jazz recording artist. He seemed to be running things on faith and a prayer. During her first week Claire and Herman had met for an hour twice. She'd moved ahead as he had directed, and three weeks later, with his nod, she was elevated to an executive with full voice, editorial license, and a budget. Wow!

Herman actually leaned in to listen when Claire spoke, and he wasn't deaf that she could discern. "Exactly!" he'd say when she would suggest next steps. For the past month she had occupied another universe, one she had only imagined.

Herman moved quickly in business, as he also moved quickly in physical space. His mannerisms were twitchy, full of energy. In conversation she sensed that she had his full attention, but at the exact right moment he would lightly interject, making connections, adjusting ideas, nothing taken for granted. That first week she had wondered, did he ever sleep?

The others in the office (all men except a female art director and Herman's secretary) seemed devoted to him; the cult following of a founder or something else? No bullshit, no sidelong glances, no phony pretense, and no apparent brown-nosing at the weekly meetings. And, so far, no glances at her blouse that she had discerned, or pats on her backside (or anywhere else). No sense of in or out of the club among the execs, no fraternity! Any name dropping had to do with the musicians and studios, agents, attorneys, and account executives. Nothing personal outside the game of launching careers and making deals for up-and-coming musicians. Of course, she was being naïve, right?

Was that him?

The man standing at the maître d's desk had recently shaved and had a new summer haircut. A navy jacket over one arm, he raised the other to wave at Claire and started to wade toward the table.

"Great to see you! Sorry I'm late." Alan started to lean over to embrace Claire but thought better of it. When he had first seen the message with the invitation to lunch he'd felt a small thrill, but this morning when he'd looked at his calendar, he'd thought of cancelling. The lineup of meetings—the thing with TransUS—and a cheery call from Wally about his new spot at Baker and Dodge, left him feeling rudderless. Maybe lunch with Claire, the good-looking gal who had become a lady executive in a world he knew a little something about, peripherally at least, would lift him out of his mood. He could give her some pointers and her smile would add to his day. Could he tell her he had started looking?

"The power went out on the six train and we were stuck in the dark between platforms for—gee, it felt like... Well, I'm glad you're still here! You look wonderful!"

A different waiter approached, a white apron wrapped around his slim waist in the custom of a good Italian trattoria. He filled their glasses, explained the cold and hot lunches, and left them to review their heavy black menus.

"So, Decca is it? Their New York office? Are you settling in?" Alan had folded his menu and took a long drink of water.

"Yes! It has been a whirlwind, but I'm keeping up. Last week I met the current and former first chairs of the Philadelphia Orchestra and a stand-in drummer for The Who."

"The Who? Who's The Who?" Alan meant it, he had never heard of the group.

"You need to get with the times, Alan." Claire teased back, but raised an eye brow. They laughed, and he listened as she explained her ridiculous first week of work, her awe for Herman, and her amusement with her view (third floor) of bobbing heads and umbrellas streaming across Midtown each morning.

"*Ensalata mixta e pasta con funghi,* please." Claire's pronunciation was flawless.

"How's your veal *scallopini?*" Alan asked. The waiter gestured with his hands as he described the sauce of fresh garlic and herbs accompanied by pasta.

"Sounds delightful. I'll start with a side salad please."

"So, Alan, what's happening at Dunaway. Any changes?" began Claire as she moved her napkin to her lap.

"Well, we hired a lady art director."

"Over sixty?" Claire replied, but Alan missed the jab.

"No, actually, a recent Pratt grad. Reserved, but seems super competent. Charlie likes her—he's the art director I mostly work with." He took a piece of bread from the basket on the table and continued, "So, tell me about the music business."

As the waiter served their starters, Claire explained the process she was learning, record album design, copyright law, editing, album distribution, and working with broadcast networks. He could see she was all over it. She beamed with confidence.

"All my music publishing experience and the semesters of college radio are paying off, Alan."

They ate for a few quiet moments. Then Claire looked up and asked, "How has work been for you lately? You didn't seem so keen on things a month ago when we went to Staten Island."

"Where to start?"

"That doesn't sound so good."

"It's been exciting, I'll say that much," he began. "I did some television work in LA for a week, and we've been writing for grocery chains, airlines, and, uh, Seagrams, actually..." He raised his eyebrows and smiled to suggest the side benefits of working on a hard liquor account, but privately, he thought, and *two* dog food campaigns!

"But, actually Claire..."

She noticed how Alan was looking across the restaurant and through the far window.

"I feel like in the last few weeks I have looked behind the curtain and seen Oz. The agency business itself, maybe it's Dunaway, my agency. I'm just not—how to put this? I think I need a change." Where had this come from? he thought. He had felt her joy as she described her job and realized the contrast between them: he couldn't stop himself.

Unintentionally Claire made a skeptical face.

"Are you pulling my leg?" she asked, not sure what to think. She was pretty sure Alan was more than all the bravado and one-liners he produced, but she wasn't sure why he was saying this to her, and why now?

Alan had his mouth full and couldn't answer.

"I think you're serious, and I'm surprised." She took a sip of water. "So, if I remember right, you are a creative supervisor? Pretty enviable spot!"

"No shit—pardon me," he responded, wiping his mouth. "J Dunaway is one of the three biggest agencies in the US. And, like all the other schmucks, I had a plan to climb the company ladder. Creative director, that was the destination—seemed unreachable when I was in the mailroom."

He took another bite. "But then what?" he continued. "I've certainly moved up, but now friends of mine, stalwarts like me, are starting to jump ship, looking for more excitement or something. Even a month or so ago I thought they were nuts. I have been here almost ten years, and you know what? It shows." He was thinking about Dick Fields. "I see every crack in the paint, if you know what I mean. And I wonder if I'm losing my edge."

"Well," began Claire. His short speech had given her time to eat most of her lunch. "What do they say once they get to their new jobs, these friends who have left Dunaway?"

"They say things are good, 'groovy.' But you know, it is hard to tell. We all want you to think we are on top, right? And agency guys are pretty good bullshitters. So, I don't know what to think."

"I'm not sure I am the right person to give you a pep talk on staying or going from your job. I'm a decade behind you—"

"Now I wouldn't go that far!" Alan interrupted. Claire smiled and conceded his point, gesturing with her glass of water.

"Well," she continued. "I fell into something by word of mouth. I was working at *Glamour*, as you know, but looking. Looking for a while—looking in all the wrong places maybe."

"Sorry."

"No need to apologize. I wouldn't have said that a week ago—about the wrong places. But I probably—no, certainly—would have been miserable at an ad agency. But, Alan, this new job! I am going to get to learn all about the business of music, agents, trends, what's hot—probably some pretty obscure acts at first, but then!" she said, shrugging her shoulders and grinning with possibility.

"Good for you, Claire." He meant it.

"So, here's the thing," she said, shifting gears, thinking more like a friend would. "You can decide to start looking, can't you? Quietly. Talk to people?"

Although he'd already started calling people, having Claire suggest it suddenly made him feel exposed, embarrassed, like he'd revealed way too much. Did he want her advice? If he didn't expect her advice, he asked himself, why the confessional?

"The gossip will fly," Alan murmured, thinking of some way to divert the conversation. He placed his cloth napkin on the table beside his plate. Claire felt the sudden awkwardness and knew immediately the nature of her blunder but stayed the course. Guys are such dolts, she thought.

"Maybe that's good!" she offered. "Make them wonder. Use it to your advantage!"

Alan signaled to the waiter that they needed the check.

"Interesting thinking," he said, turning back to her. "I very much appreciate it. But I just noticed the time," he said, indicating at his watch.

He insisted on paying.

Outside, Alan took Claire's hand. There wasn't the slightest flirtation in his gesture.

"Claire, you are not like anyone else. I'm thrilled for you. And you sure give a guy a great pep talk! I mean it."

"Well, thank you for listening to me gush! We'll see how long it lasts, right?" They laughed, and before she turned away, sunglasses on and a small wicker hat on her head, she said, "Let me leave you with a thought, okay Alan? Does it have to be another agency? Your next move? Think about that."

She turned to head across town.

"I'll see you, Alan!"

He watched her disappear into the color and movement of people trying to avoid car bumpers as they crossed the street. He adjusted his jacket over his arm and took a deep breath of warm city air. He hadn't asked her directly; he'd meant to say—why not?—keep an ear out for me. But it had suddenly felt too pathetic to ask her to help him, like Bill was doing.

She was so full of the kind of energy and attitude he wanted—and he felt some of it now, her sense of possibility.

At the corner a short man with a large mustache sold Italian ices from his cart under a striped umbrella. Alan took a lemon ice and headed back to work, grateful for the lunch and an important ally.

25

Alan, Buck, and Charlie Ogden, Dunaway's art director for Tran-sUS, arrived at Dick Field's office exactly at eleven thirty Wednesday morning. Alan prided himself on being prompt. As the head of Y&R once said, if someone comes in late every day, he better be awfully good.

"Hello, Alan." Fields had another smoke stack in his mouth, fortunately unlit. He looked at Buck and then down at Buck's boots. "What's Audie Murphy doing here?"

"Dick Fields, you know Buck Jones? He's the junior man on this."

"Here to listen and learn. Yep!" Buck said, putting on his best Central Colorado twang.

Fields shook his head. "Did you reserve the screening room?"

"Yes," Alan replied. "We have it from eleven thirty to twelve."

Suddenly, Alan became aware of the aluminum foil packages spread all over a small coffee table next to the Sloane-style wingback chair in the corner of Field's office.

"Is that lunch, Dick?"

"Yes," Fields answered, lighting the cigar.

"Is anybody going to take the foil off the food?"

"What do you mean?"

"Dick, it looks a little tacky for a couple of prospective clients, who are former pilots themselves, and not unfamiliar with '21' and the shad with lemon sauce at Christ Cella."

"Well, you don't want the sandwiches to get stale, do you?"

Buck began coughing loudly to smother a laugh and sat down hard on a swivel chair. Charlie turned his back. Alan looked at the alu-

135

minum foil sandwiches, packages of pickles, and the cardboard plates and plastic knives and forks. He was incredulous, but strangely, being pissed at Fields took away some of the usual pressure that came with making a presentation. This morning he'd taken one of Liddie's Valiums just in case he got into a panic.

Alan was about to say more, but Charlie sidled up to him while Fields was looking at some papers.

"Let it be his to lose, man."

Alan smiled. He looked out the window at the view of the General Electric Building. Fields doesn't even have a decent view, he thought smugly.

The telephone buzzed. Fields put his cigar down on an enormous ash tray and picked up the phone. He cupped his hand over the receiver and announced, "They're here."

Two men in tailored suits came around the corner, following Field's gray-haired secretary. She stood back smiling and gestured for them to enter the office.

Buck Jones bolted forward, reaching out his hand. "Welcome to J Dunaway Advertising, gentlemen. Darn, that's a fine tie. I'm Buck Jones, copywriter. Here you go, have a seat right over here."

"How do you do? Steve Shanley, advertising manager for TransUS, and this is Captain Bob Decker, commercial vice president." The two men shuffled around to the end of the table shaking, hands.

"This here is our creative chief, Alan Robinson, and for color we brought this guy along..."

"Hi, Charlie Ogden, art director. Very pleased to help you put together an exciting campaign."

"Bob, nice to see you again. Steve, it's a pleasure." Fields rose and reached across the table to shake hands, then sat and picked up his cigar. "Let's begin. We'd like you to get to know us, and we get to know you. Of course, we want to keep it brief because we know you're busy. We've got some lunch here, so it'll be a kind of working lunch," said Fields, looking pleased.

The two men looked over at the aluminum foil sandwiches.

"First of all," continued Fields, "as you know a lot about the agency already, what we'd like to do is talk about how we work and then show you some of the work we've done for other clients. A success story or two. We have quite a few," he chuckled.

Nobody smiled.

"So…" Fields began.

"Thanks, Dick," Decker, the VP, interrupted Fields's monologue.

"As you know, we were impressed by the agency's earlier creative work for TransUS, but today we are talking about a different business. Think of this as a whole new account. That's why I am here today. So, before we hear your pitch, I think what we'd most like to do is get an idea of who we'd be working with on our new international and domestic business travel advertising."

Here it comes, thought Alan.

"Well, Alan Robinson here, of course, will be in charge of the cre- atives. He has a—"

"Yes, but who'll be on the account on a day-to-day basis? I mean, will we meet the account team today, for example? I don't mean you have to have a police lineup, but both Steve and I would first like to meet the guy who's going to be in charge of the TransUS Airlines commercial account. That's why I'm here."

"Well, we have several men in mind. Excellent people."

Decker looked at Shanley. Alan looked out the window at the GE building. Charlie looked down.

"Dick, you mean you haven't anyone in mind yet who'll be manag- ing the business?" Alan heard the sound of disbelief in Steve Shanley's voice.

"Oh yes, I do." Dick's moment of triumph was coming.

"Well, can we meet him?" Shanley asked impatiently.

"You have, Steve. Me. I'll be the management supervisor on the ac- count for the first six months."

The room was silent for what seemed longer than the time it took Dick Fields to light his cigar.

Bob Decker zipped closed a small leather briefcase he had started to open shortly after sitting down at Fields's office table. That's it, Alan thought.

"What about after the first six months, Dick?" asked Steve Shanley.

Shanley, the advertising manager, the guy who had set this all up on the company end, was trying to politely salvage the meeting. He was embarrassed for himself. He had selected Dunaway as one of three finalist ad agencies to receive the TransUS business. His boss now sat across from him, zipping his briefcase. The decision had been made.

"As I said, we have several top account guys under consideration."

Fields reached over to his desk to pick up a folder. His pen went skittering across the table onto the floor. Inside the folder were files on several account supervisors Fields had singled out for the assignment. He pulled them out.

"Dick, I don't think going through the resumes of people we won't be able to meet today makes much sense." Decker was already on his feet.

"I hope you will excuse me; I can't stay for lunch. I'm sure you and Alan and his talented team here will run Steve through the things you've planned. Nice to meet you, Alan. Steve, I'll see you back at the office after, uh… lunch."

The office door closed, and Buck rose to his feet before Alan could say anything. Charlie looked like he needed a smoke, while Dick Fields looked like he was trying to figure out what had just happened.

Just like that, Buck took over. "Well, damn! How 'bout that, Steve? TransUS just got lucky. Looks like you'll have Dunaway's premier account management service, headed up by Mister Fields himself! Betcha *Ad Age* will be talkin' about that in a week or two."

Steve smiled. He seemed slightly confused by Buck's outburst but enjoying his native charm.

"But right here is the creative team," Buck continued, indicating the others.

"The best, most versatile, creative advertising team in New York. And we are dedicated to your campaign. Dedicated! We have an exceptional presentation for you. TransUS is gonna fly high with corporate passengers if ya'll choose Dunaway."

Alan shook his head slightly and gestured with his eyes at Fields. Buck got the hint.

"But we have to hold on a little sec, because I think maybe Dick here wants you to have a bite to eat before we head into the viewing room. Am I right, Dick?"

"Uh, sure," replied Fields.

Alan rose and passed out the sandwiches.

Dick Fields re-lit his cigar and began peeling off aluminum foil from his sandwich and pickle. Steve tried to peek inside to see what his was, getting mayonnaise on his fingers.

Alan looked at the GE Building, thinking. He'd make the pitch with Buck. But he'd lead, not Buck, or they'd scare this guy away. But it was really beyond his control. Do your part and be done, pal, he thought to himself. He took a bite of his roast beef on rye. Maybe he didn't have to be at this agency anymore.

* * *

The next day was Thursday. Around ten, Alan was at his desk reading *The New York Times* and having a cup of instant coffee when the phone rang.

"Mister Robinson?" an older lady's voice inquired.

"Yes."

"It's Mr. Fields."

Alan waited for Fields to come on the phone.

"Good morning, Alan."

"Morning, Dick. What's up?

"We didn't get the TransUS business. Just got the call from Steve. It went to Y& R."

"No shit, Dick. No shit. Well, chalk that one up."

"I think next time you should handle the pitch yourself, Alan. Not sure it came across that favorably to have a junior person deliver to such an important client. Your man certainly didn't have your, uh, finesse."

"Stop right there, Fields." Alan had made some decisions that week. He was looking at the trade papers, and he'd called his friend Bill Taylor again.

"You just take care of things over in account management, okay? Find another account to lose, Dick. And next time you need work over here, there might be a long wait."

He hung up the phone, threw down his pencil, grabbed his jacket, and headed for the elevator.

Time for a lemon ice.

* * *

Later that afternoon, Doris was preparing to type a memo, feeding a sandwich of paper and blue carbon paper into her typewriter, when the handsome office boy approached with his cart. He handed her the mail. After sorting through it, Doris rose from her desk in the secretary pool and walked over to Alan's office door. She tapped on his name plate with her newly painted red finger nails.

"Come!" replied Alan's dry voice from within. Doris opened the door.

"What have we here? You look scholarly!" she said, grinning at Alan.

"Some fascinating reading, compliments of the Dunaway Research Department," he smirked, looking up from a pile of white paper memos and colorful, shiny, bound documents.

Alan welcomed the distraction. He had just been trying to read this stack of "reports" on dog food: statistics on American dog ownership among families compared to single people, the regional distribution of dog breeders, canned versus dry dog food sales and distribution, and, of course, brand endorsements by veterinarians. He had a meeting at two with the K-9 Rations account rep.

Doris glanced at the report covers and smiled.

"Looks like delicious reading. Here, today's mail." She placed the pile of envelopes and newspapers on his desk.

"Thanks."

"Sure," she said as she backed out the door. To Alan it sounded like "shoe-ah." He smiled.

On top of the folded weekly trade papers were a few long white envelopes. He opened the one with the neatly handwritten address.

A small piece of Decca Records notepaper was inside with a typed note.

Alan,

If you get a call from somebody named Sam Delafield, take it!

Claire

Intriguing. He had been calling people all week, quietly asking around about which agencies were looking for creative supervisors. He waited to make his calls until late afternoon when his team had gone to their corners, probably on the phone themselves looking for their next move. Most days after four thirty Doris typed up his correspondence. And on Tuesdays and Thursdays she left early to take care of some relative—her Aunt? He wasn't sure. That was the best time to avoid her notice.

Who was Sam Delafield? No doubt a music executive or some kind of head-hunter.

Funny. Claire had got him thinking. Since their lunch he had been noticing things the way you do when you learn a new word; you suddenly see it everywhere. Like yesterday, he'd been out on Long Island at Media Sound for the recording of the Lucky Stores jingle. By the men's room he had found himself reading announcements, news bits, and job postings on their in-house bulletin board. Then, on Friday, he went against his own rules about trade papers—"Weren't all trade papers actually storefronts for personnel agencies?" Tom liked to sneer—and bought *Billboard* and another couple of music business rags from the news kiosk at Grand Central.

The articles in the various publications sounded a lot like *Ad Age*: the upcoming movie soundtrack awards, recording studio acquisitions, everyone trying to explain why musicians switch labels; but he found himself pretty interested. Then, just this morning, jostling along on the subway, he had caught himself reading an article over the shoulder of the guy next to him. A whole column on the wheeling and dealing involved with various New York Philharmonic recordings. Juicy stuff, apparently.

I guess the music biz is my new distraction, he thought, turning back to the American Pet Products Association data. Forty eight percent of Americans would own pets in twenty years. Dog food would be a billion-dollar industry before the end of the decade.

"Do I really care?" he thought. "Yes, I do. Right now, I have to care so we get the business!" He lifted the last sharp pencil out of his cup and began to take notes.

26

Thursday night, the second week of August. Alan turned the heavy key in the dead bolt. Opening the door to the apartment felt like stepping into a church sanctuary. He breathed in the comforting smell of home: smoky carpet, furniture polish, mildew, and the faint bouquet of used coffee grounds. The silver framed mirror hung centered over the black, front-hall chest. A jumble of mail spilled over in the basket. His keys jingled as he dropped them on the tray. The knowing voice of the creaky oak floor boards as he crossed the threshold into the living room.

"Hi, sweetheart."

Liddie rose from the two-seater sofa, unlit cigarette in hand. Alan stopped still, jolted out of his mindless routine. Today's paper folded in his left hand dropped to the floor.

"Lid! It's Thursday. What a surprise!"

She stood coyly smiling but uncertain. He picked up the paper and placed it in the mail basket.

"I have news."

"News? What kind of news? Jesus!" Alan sputtered, kissing her on the cheek and taking a step back. "Hang on. I need to take a leak. The train uptown took forever." Alan dove down the hall, still in his street shoes.

* * *

Liddie knew this part would be hard. Alan didn't like surprises. She knew coming into the city was off-script, but she was desperate. How long had it been since she'd been in the apartment in August?

Probably since Clem was born, and he was eight now. Years. Water under the bridge, she told herself.

She put down the cold cigarette, smoothed her hair, and straightened her blouse. Her lime-green slacks were rumpled from the train.

The weekend before had clarified everything. All summer Alan had complained about going with her to club functions, preferring to sit home at the breezy house overlooking the harbor and listen to baseball on the radio. Of course, that wasn't the whole of it. He willingly minded the boys; he doted on them. He volunteered on the dock with their weekend sailing races, and if he came up on Thursday nights, he watched them try to hit the ball at their Friday tennis lessons at the club. Alan always put the boys to bed. But most of her and Alan's evenings together were spent with a drink and a book. His absence from her life—their summer weekend life—was complete. Nothing had changed. Till recently.

Most weeks she spent lots of time on the phone scheduling each weekend so it would be full of distractions, perfectly balanced with time for friends and family excursions to the beach. She planned pretty cocktail parties, arranging the terrace with flowers and trays of hors d'oeuvres. And she accepted invites—only the ones she thought he'd enjoy. Yet he always insisted they go in two cars, and of course she was left to apologize when he left early. It wasn't unlike their life in the city, she had realized.

After her escapade earlier in the summer, she had avoided having a big talk with Alan; a confrontation would upend everything, and she couldn't see how they would work through it. Their life was comprised of two-day couplets between five days of uncertain silence.

So, she had settled back in, going along like she always had, till last weekend. Friday night driving to Pequot from the train, completely out of the blue, Alan had announced he would like to go to the club dinner dance. He had even dressed up!

Saturday night they danced, and he joked around. Later, the sex was thrilling—unlike him—slow and affectionate and creative in ways that embarrassed her to think about—but she loved to think about! On Sunday morning when she went down and made the coffee, she was certain of one thing. He had probably just come out of another relationship.

She had sensed it without knowing for certain, that there was something going on back in Manhattan. Maybe that was why the whole summer she had been angry. He was indifferent, so in response, she had become hyper-organized, controlling, tight lipped, and resentful.

"My God," she had said a month ago to her cousin Coleen. "In the evenings back in New York I have nothing to say to Alan. He's not interested in what Clem's teacher said or how our building's holiday decorating is coming along. To him, nothing I have to say is the least bit important. To him it's like, so what? And he seems to have given up trying to tell me anything—the news from work, new accounts, work gossip. Then in the summer, the few times he comes to the country on Thursday nights, he's tired, and I drag him to the cookout. He doesn't want to go, but I want to go! And so, we start every weekend mad at each other. I'm terrible company, but he's worse. It's all built up. We have nothing to say."

Then, three weeks ago, Liddie had started to work on her plan. She needed a way forward. Things were going to be different because she had finally woken up. She didn't want to end her marriage, she wanted to change it. While it might mean she was the only one of her friends to do it, and that she'd have to face a lot of judgement, she was going to fix the imbalance; she was going to find a part-time job!

So, Sunday morning she had made him breakfast, taken him to the train as usual, and let him leave without telling him her big news—she had an actual job offer.

It had to be lonely in the hot apartment all summer, she thought now, looking around the living room, the record albums on the floor, the socks by the chair, the book he was reading—what was it? *The Captain*, another military novel—on the table beside his big chair. She lit her cigarette. Does he also feel alone during the school year when we're both in the city? Like I do?

Liddie was standing by the record player when he came into the room, her smoldering cigarette in the glass ash tray. She stared at him with a look that was hard to read, sad? Was she waiting for him to say something? He was suddenly alert, aware of her facing him, her familiar narrow body, her chest rising and falling. He unbuttoned his collar and pulled off his tie, a diversionary move, trying to seem at ease.

"Would you like a drink, Alan, before I go on?" Liddie launched past him.

"Sure. Uh, but actually, we don't have much. No limes, maybe an old lemon. Tonic, but no soda water."

In the kitchen Liddie took a metal ice tray from the freezer, reached for the glasses, and then stood still, a glass in each hand. She placed them on the cutting board and leaned against the counter, breathing hard. Slow down, she thought. Just breathe a minute, in and out. Slow it down. This is good. The rest doesn't matter.

Her heart was pounding. She straightened up. She wrenched the cold handle of the metal ice tray and the cubes dropped into the glasses, "clunk clunk." They frosted immediately. She sliced what she could from the moldy lemon, poured in the gin and then the tonic. It fizzed; the tiny droplets danced on the ice and spraying her hand as she picked them up.

Liddie entered the living room with two tall, frosty glasses.

"So, what is the surprise? Something with the boys?" Sitting in his green armchair, Alan took both drinks. Liddie turned and pulled the blue upholstered swivel chair from its place by the TV so close their knees could touch.

This was different, he thought. He got ready to feel accused.

"Well, no, this is my news," she said, taking a sip.

"Wait, are you trying to tell me…?"

"No, no. I am not pregnant. And I'm going to try and not be mad that that's the first thing you thought of!"

"Sorry, babe. Go on."

Alan wasn't sure how this was going to go. He twirled an ice cube in his drink with his index finger. The first sip of the cold drink warmed him up.

"So, a few weeks ago I played tennis with Alita Lewis. You know her, right?

"Not the gal who plays braless? Married to the *Newsweek* reporter? Who doesn't!"

"I know what you're thinking, not my typical doubles partner. Well, I had signed up for a ladies tennis ladder."

"Not exactly one of the ladies… Anyway, sorry. Go on."

"Well, afterward they had some iced tea in the tennis shack, and we were talking. She had heard about my interest in fabrics—someone told her about the help I gave Coleen with their living room and the others. You know, how I found that little place in Providence that imports fabrics and cushions from Italy—"

He nodded vaguely. He had no idea about any of this. He loved her sense of style and color, though.

"Well, Alita is launching an import business. She lives here in the city; her kids go to Friends, apparently."

"One of those."

"Alan!" They both chuckled. She took a sip from her drink.

"Go on." Alan patted her knee. He liked the feeling of being on the same wavelength.

"She has an office in the city and a warehouse."

"Okay?"

"Well, she needs an assistant! Someone with interiors experience. So, I wrote a resumé. We met last week in Pequot, and I met her designer, Suneeta—"

"Not a Club member, I guess."

"Alan, be serious. I have a job! That's it. Part-time, of course. I start the week school starts."

He had to admit, he was caught off guard.

"I'm in town because I have an onboarding interview. Well, they called it that. She hired me! I still can't believe it."

"Wow." He took a drink. A lot was swirling in his head. His latest confrontation with Dick Fields and today's subsequent conversation with his boss, Lou. His disgust with the advertising business. His own confusion about what was next for him. The note from Claire, Claire! And Lina. He flinched with the momentary image of Wally's office in a dream he'd had.

"What do you think, honey?" Liddie was beaming at him now.

"I guess I think it's great. I'm surprised. Wait, when exactly did this all transpire?" Alan had not seen this coming. Was this what amnesia felt like, or a blackout? Since May he'd been with Lina—and then trying to get Lina out of his system since early July. Then California. Admit it, your head is up your ass! Had Liddie asked him to use his portable typewriter a few weeks ago?

"You didn't talk about this last weekend. Why didn't you say something?"

"Wel—" She smiled in a soft, knowing, cat-eyed way.

"No, don't answer that. Last weekend was really nice. It felt… Lid, you seem so excited. It's good, but, uh… it's just a change. A big change." He paused. "You haven't wanted a job for long, have you? Have you tried to tell me this? I always thought you were fine as a stay-at-home Mom."

"Well, I was…" she began, but Alan continued.

"It's just…" he tried. "This makes me wonder where I've been. I mean, not really! It seems a little out of thin air, though. It makes me feel a little like, I guess—do you want to get some dinner somewhere?"

She noticed that Alan had turned beet-red. Was it the drink? He'd finished his already. But as he looked away and got up from his chair, she recognized his vulnerability. He didn't like being exposed. Did he feel exposed? He did better when he was in command of the conversation, in charge. She knew that about him.

But she felt his support; he hadn't questioned the job itself. She wasn't going to doubt herself in front of him (although of course she doubted everything about this), she wasn't going to ask for permission. She had to meet him where he liked to be, in charge, but in charge herself as well. Like they had been in '53. That's where she wanted to be again. Both of them working, both paid, both knowing people, both busy, both a little out of reach—that had been a very sexy time. They would figure out the kids, hire a part-time nanny.

The humidity was suddenly oppressive. Liddie never perspired, but she did now. She put down her drink. The rest could wait for later, or tomorrow. Before she went back to Pequot, they'd lay it all out, all of it, and reassemble their marriage, she hoped.

"I crave Chinese. There's no Chinese in Pequot! Let's go to the Lotus."

By the door, Alan turned to her with keys in his hand and a big smile.

"Come here." He pulled her in for a hug and then looked at her. Was that relief he saw? They kissed long and affectionately, only stopping when she started to laugh.

"Come on," she said, and opened the door. He pressed for the elevator.

27

Alan leaned over Liddie and kissed her forehead. He was dressed and shaved. She lay half-out of the sheets. The air was already sticky. Her hair fell across the pillow. To him, she looked seventeen.

"I wish you didn't have to go, Alan. It's been so long since we talked like we did last night. I don't want it to stop."

"Neither do I." He kissed her again. He was cross-eyed from lack of sleep, would have loved to fall in beside her, but he had to get to a meeting.

"You love me?" she asked.

"Yes, I love you."

"No more screwing around?"

"No more screwing around."

"Would you like a Jack Shepherd Pie next Friday night?"

"More than anything."

"Do you like being married to me?" She blurted it out.

Alan reached for his briefcase. "You have to get going there, lady. You have an appointment with your new boss, Mrs. Robinson."

"Alan, answer the question."

"Yes. But do you like being married to me, is the question?" Alan sat beside her on the bed.

"I didn't think I did, but I want to be married to you. I want our marriage to work."

"Well, that's what I want too, more than anything, " he said, looking straight at her, his eyes welling up. "I'm sorry, honey. I have been an idiot. Like I said last night, being alone in the city in the summer is no good. All those stories I told you are true. Somehow, we have to do it differently, you and I. Because the way things are, leave a guy in New York for three months in this scene and you have problems."

He brushed the wisps of blonde hair across her forehead and behind her ear.

"Let's make this our new phase—a new inning! Let's try, Alan." She turned and looked at the red clock. "Yikes it's nine!" she said, sitting up.

"And I have to get to my office so I don't get fired before we start the next inning." He turned back at the bedroom door. "Who knows? We didn't talk about everything last night. We have more to cover. Maybe I'll have a new job too pretty soon! Bye, hun. Break a leg!"

He fled down the hall.

* * *

"Good morning, Mr. Harris," Alan said cheerily as he passed the security desk at 666 5th Avenue.

"Crazy troubled times, ain't they?" murmured Mr. Harris, the building guard, as he put down his copy of the *New York Post* and lifted his hand to acknowledge Alan.

"Yes sir, they certainly are," Alan replied. He had scanned the *Times* this morning. Mayhem again in Harlem, more chaos than even the *Post* could shout about; 380,000 American troops in South Vietnam; Federal troops called in to quell the anger and looting in Detroit; fires burning in cities across the US.

However, by the time the elevator doors opened on his floor, J Dunaway Advertising, he'd forgotten all that.

"Good morning, Mr. Robinson!" He loved walking along the outside wall toward his office, the secretaries in their cubicles all smiling and cheerful.

"Good morning, Alan!" Doris was ready with a cup of coffee by the time he made it to his door. She followed him and handed him some pink notes.

"A couple of phone messages for you. Also, today's meeting about the Prell presentation has been moved to eleven, and the Johnson Wax account meeting is at three. Landon already stopped in. Anything you need from me?"

Alan was looking at the messages: one from Sam Delafield. It would have to wait till later.

* * *

Settled in his office after debriefing with his team—the floor wax meeting had taken a good turn and the client liked the boards—Alan sipped on a Coke, studying the pink phone message slip, phone to his ear.

"This is Sam Delafield."

Alan raised an eyebrow. This guy answered his own phone!

"Hello, Sam. This is Alan Robinson over at J Dunaway Advertising. I had a note that you called?"

"Yes, Alan. Thanks for getting back to me so fast! I got your name from Wally Hendricks over at Baker and Dodge. I helped him this summer in LA arranging studio musicians for some of his accounts. I work for Verve Records representing some artists. Wally and I got talking, and he said I should call you."

"He's a good man. Likes to have fun!" Alan hadn't phoned Wally yet to tell him he was looking—he couldn't face the ridicule. But maybe Alan was wrong. It sounded like maybe Wally was looking out for him.

"Alan, is this a good time to talk?"

"Well, it depends. What's this about? Do you have something to offer Dunaway?" Alan played it cool. He really didn't know what this was about, but because of Claire's note, he had suspicions.

"Actually, I have a question for you. We are looking to hire someone like you. If my timing is wrong, say the word. But if you don't mind, could I take you to lunch on Monday?"

"Wow. No. I mean, yes. Monday's good. Thanks for the invitation. Any place in mind?"

"How about Italian? A quiet place I know on 3rd and 50th called Tomaldo's.[8] The best chicken *picatta* in town."

"Okay, Sam. See you then." What d'ya know?

It was later than he thought. Alan picked up his one-suiter suitcase and put it on his desk. He flipped the latches, opened the bag and pushed a few shirts and books to one side. From the small brown refrigerator by his desk, he took out a can of beer and put it in the suitcase. He had just enough time to take a cab to Grand Central to catch the 5:20 to New London.

Alan figured the train was going to be packed, but he made it in enough time to find a coach seat on the side with the nicer view. Soon, the Block Island crowd began stumbling and shoving through the coaches.

Alan was reading the *New York Post* and had just opened the beer. He looked at the growing horde of passengers and hoped that nobody would ask to sit next to him. Just then he spotted a beautiful woman at the far end of the coach. She was tan. Her dress was rust and yellow, a short skirt. Her honey hair pulled back just the way he liked it. He returned to the *Post* knowing full well who would be sitting beside him all the way to New Haven.

"Is anyone sitting here?" came a soft female voice. Alan looked up.

"Hi Lid! What a treat."

28

He arrived at the restaurant a little early. Instead of waiting inside or under the awning, he continued around the block, walking up 3rd Avenue and turning the corner toward Lexington. Might as well stretch my legs.

Following a massive storm over the weekend, the air was cool and breezy. The city felt renewed, like someone had washed the windows. But the sun was still hot, and he loosened his tie as he rounded the corner back to the restaurant.

"Alan?" A short man in dark glasses waved as he leaned in to pay his cab. He had curly dark brown hair, fashionably long, and wore a navy shirt, sleeves rolled up. He carried a thin briefcase.

They entered into a dark vestibule, passing through heavy velvet curtains into the muffled dining room. The formally dressed, neatly bearded, portly maître d took them to their corner table.

"That's the son. Mr. Tomaldo Senior works evenings," said Sam, removing his dark glasses. This was clearly one of his spots. They sat and adjusted themselves to the air conditioning, both reaching for their water glasses.

"So, have you been in the city long this trip?" Alan began.

"I actually moved back to New York in July to—"

"I bet you miss LA!"

"Sure. I forgot what a steam room New York can be!"

"Sorry. Go on…"Alan felt nervous.

"Well, as I was saying, I moved back to the city to start a new division of our company. As I think I told you on the phone, I'm a producer; I help a musician record what I believe—and they hope—will be a great record album. In the last couple years, I have worked with Buddy Rich, Lee Konitz, Natalie Cole—"

"Some of the greats."

"Direct work. In the studio, that's the fun stuff. But now, because of some successes across the company—big successes—I am having to handle more at the business end. Things have exploded."

"Sounds like a 'good problem,' as they say."

The waiter delivered a basket of Italian bread and butter, filled their glasses, and took their orders. Small glass bottles of golden olive oil and red wine vinegar sat beside an unlit candle at the center of the table.

"So, it has been a good year," Sam continued. "We just launched a whole new sound—not me, but our group. I'm sure you have heard of this album with Getz and Gilberto?"

"*Girl from Ipanema*. Incredible. I'm a student of Stan Getz."

"Well, good. That's really good to hear." Sam paused to bite a piece of warm, crusty bread he had dipped in olive oil. "Why don't I get right to the point? I'm looking for someone with studio musician connections, who knows audiences, but who also knows branding, has some business chops, and would like to make it big as an A&R man—someone who can follow these new sounds, follow the right sounds. We want to lead the industry with new hip music, new jazz.

"Alan?"

Alan must have been staring. He took a deep breath.

"Uh, yeah. A&R, that's artist and repertoire, right? That's being the creative mastermind working with new musicians. Huh. Seems like there must be lots of guys on the inside you can pick from. But, judging from your face, maybe not!"

"We are throwing a wide net."

"I'm sure I can make some inquiries—I know some superb talent in the agency business." Alan deflected what was pretty obvious—but for some reason he had a hard time believing—he was being recruited. Those old nerves were flaring up. Alan's heart was hammering. His grandfather's voice *"What have you always loved, Alan? Do that, son! Don't be a working stiff like me."* He could feel his face redden. Be cool, Alan. Hear what this guy has to say.

The waiter brought their drinks. Sam had a coke, and, taking his cue, Alan ordered soda with lemon.

Sam lowered his voice as if he were sharing a confidence.

"So, I'll lay it on you straight, Alan. We lost a couple of guys to small labels—the R&B scene, soul, that sort of thing. And that lead me to call my old friend, Herman Warner, who you may have heard of…?

"He's up there at Decca I think, er, I read about him in one of the trade papers. Or maybe it was *Billboard*." Herman? Of course. Claire worked for him.

"Ah, you read *Billboard*."

"Yeah. I hate the gossip, but I follow a few careers, a few horn players I once knew."

"So, Herman, 'no bullshit Herman,' he's an old friend, tells me I need someone like him, someone who served our country—but not *this* fucking war, one of the earlier ones, so not too young. Preferably a musician.

"When Herman has an idea, he's usually right. So, he mentioned checking out the big agencies, like Dunaway, Y&R, and Baker and Dodge. 'Ask around,' he said. 'Find out who's tired of making soap commercials.' Gotta love Herman!

"Anyway, a guy I spoke to tells me you played in Germany after the big show."

"Yes, and played summer clubs in PA before that, nothing too serious."

Alan was thinking about the smoky living room in Scranton, Pennsylvania, where he and some friends recorded on his friend's uncle's reel-to-reel fifteen years ago. What ever happened to that?

"Alan, here's the thing. We need to ride this success, which means moving fast and thinking differently. Verve just bought a catalogue of jazz and soul albums from a small label called CLT, owned by an old friend in the business who made his name at Bethlehem Records. He's since 'moved on,' as they say. I think it's a gold mine. Does any of this sound interesting to you, Alan?"

"I'm flattered. My head is spinning a little, actually. I have to tell you, working with studio musicians is the best part of the job at Dunaway. We recorded a session with The Fifth Dimension in March."

"They are a really tight group," Sam said, switching his demeanor.

"Of course," he continued. "I'll say this now. We could meet your salary—meet it. But this job is not a big moneymaker, well, till it is! You know what I mean?"

"Wait, you haven't even seen my resumé."

The waiter returned with oval plates of food. A pungent balsamic steam of warm oregano and garlic filled their senses.

"Enjoy!" the waiter chirped, looking approvingly at the two men who had forks in hand. There was long moment for what Alan would describe later to others as 'ecstasy of the mouth.' This was remarkable Italian cooking.

"Pretty good, right?" Sam said while chewing.

"I'm speechless."

"This is how I reel you in." They both laughed.

"I hope you'll give this some thought. When you have, we can discuss formalities. But for now, how would you like to come meet the New York Verve people and see how it feels?"

"Name the time and I'll be there."

* * *

Alan decided to walk from the Lexington Avenue subway over to Park and uptown to their apartment. It was a clear night, a few stars just visible beyond the glass cloche of light over the city. September 5th, middle of the week. Tomorrow the kids come back to the city.

What an evening. He'd been a little self-conscious when Tom had proposed a gathering. He had wanted to duck out without a fuss. The less said the better because, let's face it, he was scared shitless to leave Dunaway and advertising, the world he knew.

His plan had been to keep in touch with his team but hope that time blurred the memory of his swift exit with other people. But Tom insisted, and, as it turned out, it was a hell of an evening. People showed up: you'd think he was moving overseas or something. He was deeply touched.

Tom chose to have it in the big back room at Dewey's. He knew that was Alan's spot. Those spare ribs with duck sauce were Alan's idea of heaven.

Wally came; he was the first one there. What a shocker that was. He said he had just returned from a vacation to the coast that turned out to be a two-week 'retreat' with his wife. He said he'd never experienced anything like it.

"Alan, it was transformative. I realized this life I am leading is not what I am meant to do," he declared without irony.

"Are you sure it wasn't something you smoked out there?"

"You can laugh, but, well, Adelle and I have been in psychotherapy."

"I'm sorry."

"No man, it's the best thing that's ever happened. Don't let anybody tell you therapy is for losers. I've been a bum. But this place in California, it's called Eseline, right on the coast, it's magnificent. And not just the view."

Alan had never heard Wally use the word 'magnificent' about anything. And, under the recessed lighting, the man looked younger, smiling benignly, as if he didn't have an answer for any of it.

People had entered the room then, and they had turned to greet their friends. Later when things had thinned out—Wally was one of the last to leave, and he hadn't touched anything more powerful than soda water—he handed Alan a small package. It was a smooth, black rock. Alan felt it now in his pocket. A little bit of Wally's awakening.

Unlike Wally, Alan had had a couple of drinks, so the evening air was helping to clear his head. He remembered that he had promised to pick up some staples at the market. His watch said eight fifteen. The sun was behind the buildings, a rose cast rimming the clouds, and some of the windows high above the street ahead of him were on fire. He cut over to Madison.

The big grocery store was open till nine. He went through the automatic doors and grabbed a cart. The produce area was chilly and smelled damp and sweet. Liddie would bring some fresh stuff back from the country, but he bagged some peaches and a lime and pushed the cart toward the cereal aisle, grabbing a red box of Wheat Chex. By the Maxwell House coffee he had to back up so an older guy could squeeze through the aisle from the other direction. "How do the gals do this during the day when it's busy?" he thought.

A jar of Skippy, another of strawberry jam, a bottle of Vermont Maid, some Aunt Jemima mix, a dozen eggs, OJ, milk, a loaf of Arnold bread, Schweppes, a couple of rolls of Charmin, and a tube of Crest. At the register he handed the checkout guy a twenty and waited for change.

If he hadn't been tight from the party, he might have thought to go home first and pick up Liddie's shopping cart. But he managed to carry the two paper bags, one in each arm, the few blocks back to their apartment building. He was grateful for Don, the doorman.

* * *

Alan had to admit, it was a new sensation readying the apartment for Liddie and the boys. The cleaning lady had come, and the place was sparkling. All the beds were freshly made.

In his robe and slippers, hands washed, he returned to the kitchen to assess the cupboards. Not too bad. Only one roach skittered for the corner. Into the trash he chucked a few moldy jars, some open noodles, and a buggy box of Uncle Bens.

The fridge was bright (had the light been out before?) and the shelves were clean. He filled them with the new food. It looked welcoming. Liddie would be pleased.

Drawing a glass of water from the kitchen tap—he always let it run for at least half a minute to get it really cold—he returned to the living room. He opened the windows by his chair to let in the night. Waves of noise from the street eleven stories below, voices, bus brakes, a train rumble, laughter, the hum still there even in the lulls—the rhythms that helped him unwind at night in the summer. His chair exhaled as he sat down. He smiled contentedly. Tomorrow they come.

The End

Afterword

This novel has two authors. Richard N. Anderson, the first author of this book, was my father. He worked in advertising in New York City from 1952 until 1974 when he died of suicide—only forty-six years old—in Tokyo, Japan. Many years later, when my mother died in the fall of 2000, I found typed notes for a novel my dad had started way back in the 1960s. He called it *The Summer Bachelor*. Reading the pages drove me to research and write a memoir (spiced up with some of his vignettes) that I published in 2013, *The Lost Chapters*.

After that book, I began daydreaming at work (a university research job) about doing something with the rest of the material. The scraps of paper and pages covered in pencil edits—all of it on computer by then—continued to call to me; such a trove of details about the *Madmen* era, why not try to finish the project he started? Could I do that?

I tried figuring out characters. Annoyingly, Alan would contrive a gag with some art director or copywriter, but that guy never appeared again! Several people were Alan's "best friend in the business." It was a hard puzzle, but I am persistent, especially when I'm emotionally involved, and, for obvious reasons, I was emotionally involved.

I mapped a network of ad agencies, collapsed and renamed characters, and kept editing. After a while, as the story emerged, I wrote a few chapters using some of his dialogue and the sublime detail of 1960's Midtown views and streetscapes! I did my best to imagine Alan Robinson, my dad's main character, knowing little about the fears and motivations of white men working at 666 5th Avenue in 1967.

And here is where the work with the archival material got challenging. My dad's descriptions of California business trips, New York restaurants, and certain people revealed that he'd been writing for years, maybe as long as eight years. I noticed a big contrast between the lust and fun of the short bits (written earlier) and the heavier stuff that had been retyped on finer paper stock. In the mid-1960s Benton and Bowles had paid my dad a huge salary as a creative chief to tease his team of copywriters until they came up with ideas to sell stuff. The sordid half-page bits of writing about dating newscasters came from that period—anecdotes he typed up quickly so he could remember the gag.

But then, after a few coveted promotions, 1971 found dad in management at a new agency, and not by choice. He was miserable and drinking a lot. His portrayal of the character Account Man Dick Fields says it all.

I hatched a plan to post "chapters" of what I called *An Ad Man's New York Summer: 1967*, as a serial blog; blogging was in its primordial stage. My generous, knowledgeable, and techy colleague/friend, Vic, showed me how to set up an RSS feed (very trendy!) and market to subscribers. Of course, I was working full-time, and I was too cheap to pay for help, so only about fifty friends ever read it!

I enjoyed designing my illustrated posts each week and dove in to moving the plot forward. I inserted a little empathy and self-reflection where there was none. I also added a character, Claire, and studied the Robinson's marital dilemma. But as I changed the story to head in a new direction, I had self-doubts. Was I stealing or plagiarizing? Was this *my* work?

One voice argued that the writing wouldn't have been read and enjoyed had I not messed around with it. The other voice responded that no outside editorial or legal authority was overseeing this project. I didn't have Dick Anderson's permission to change the plot and characters, especially sitting in the 21st century judging the cultural norms of the author.

I went to the William Hall Library of the Cranston Public Library to read about ghostwriting and ghostwriters who posthumously continue an author's work. I found reassurance in an article from 1980. In the *NYT*, Dudley Clendinen quoted an unnamed *Sunday Times* editor speaking about editing Henry Kissinger's biography. The editor said "It was a matter of shortening sentences, changing the order of stories, tightening up—a craftsman's job. We call it subbing here. You call it copyediting." The editor went on, "A bricklayer working to an architect's plan." I told myself that I was in the same realm, working somewhere between heavy editing and what felt like collaboration. I was reassured; writers work with original material all the time. But, lucky me, I had the pleasure of riffing off my father's humor and completing a scene he hadn't finished.

There was the psychological aspect. What was I *really* doing? As I wrote new posts, I consciously steered the plot in the direction it might have gone had the author been a spiritually healthy person. The material from the later years reeked of his alcoholism; he was cynical, disdainful of the advertising business, and bored. So, as his co-dependent collaborator, here is my confession. I wanted to show my dad how unexpectedly life can change for the better, a path forward can come into view. But without treatment for addiction, he couldn't have imagined the possibilities that were ahead for a guy like him, even with a divorce looming and plenty of bills. In 2003 his former co-workers told me that after advertising (and divorces), their lives really began; one became a sculptor, another a psychiatrist. There was actually plenty of hope to go around in the early 1970s. Of course, I wanted to save his life. To rewrite it.

Finally, I apologize to you, reader, for stereotypes repeated in this book. Also for the fetishizing of cheap sex and the sexist and demeaning attitudes that may offend the reader. I had reservations and have some shame about the sexual jokes and the slurs. But this is the material I had to work with. Should I have at least toned it down? My three aunts, who each worked in the arts and media in New York from the

1950's to the 1970's all said don't change a word, "That's what it was like."

In 2016, after the election, we moved house, and I dropped the blog project. Then #MeToo happened. I couldn't stomach even thinking about it! Then there was a pandemic we had to get through. I thought I had abandoned the unfinished blog to the ether, but one day, the domain name and website for *An Ad Man's New York Summer* came up for renewal. Rather than pay up, I downloaded the material to my computer and cancelled my subscriptions.

Now that it was in front of me again, I began thinking about Claire and Alan. I'm over sixty. If I "went off the scene," as my mother used to say, what would become of my effort? Who wants to cherish their mom's unfinished blog? (A little ironic don't you think?)

How could I move this story to a conclusion? Should Alan hit bottom? Should Claire finally get a job? Should that affect Alan? What about Liddie? Who the heck is she? How can she participate, besides (as my father had written) unblinkingly forgiving Alan's unforgivable transgressions?

I got back to it. I began to write.

I have spent over twenty years with these characters; I have had trouble delving into other writing projects as deeply. Am I co-dependent? Unethical? Obsessed? It doesn't matter. We are all drawn forward—or held back—by emotional attachments, sometimes, it seems, by forces entirely out of our control.

I hope my sons live life to the fullest and learn many lessons along the way, including that time brings perspective to pain, it allows one to find joy and humor in hard things. Writing *The Ad Man's Summer* was a way to preserve and share your grandfather's creativity and, more importantly for me, to have an honest conversation (actually numerous conversations) with him in the process. I brought Alan and Liddie through some dark questioning times to a reasonable place, a happy moment, and a life ahead full of... who knows. Maybe they'll find some meaning and reward in whatever comes next. That's what I am hoping.

January 20, 2025.

Endnotes

1. In the 1960s, a white, working-class, mostly Irish suburb of NYC located in Queens.
2. *Brother Rat* is the title of a 1938 American comedy film about novice military cadets.
3. A 'proof' is the final corrected and approved draft of an ad, and a trade proof, in this context, promotes a car to car dealers to sell.
4. TV ads for the stir-in-water tummy settler were wildly popular beginning in 1967.
5. Indonesia's dictatorship brutally suppressed a popular uprising in the 1960s. Shanker was the famous, and consequential, strong man/union president of the American Federation of Teachers (AFT).
6. The comic was Buddy Hackett.
7. Note: Excerpt from *The Lost Chapters* by Lisa Anderson, ©2013.
8. Tom Luclani from Bianca Cinque Terre, Italy, owned Tomaldo Restaurant, 3rd Ave. and 50th Street. It definitely had the best 'anything parmigiana' in NYC.

Acknowledgements

I am grateful for the stories, observations, and other writing that Dick Anderson left behind, and I am grateful to my mother, Edie, for not getting rid of them. Dad, sorry I couldn't fit it all in.

Appreciation to the following dear people for their encouragement and feedback over the years: Vic Divecha, Tory McCagg, N.T., Anne Scinta Smith, Barbara Lucas, Karl Lindholm, Mike Butler, and every one of my friends and cousins who read the blog, and thanks to the members of the Burlington Writer's Workshop, Middlebury Chapter.

Forever and always thanks to Miles for your wise edits, and thanks for being such a kind human being.

Richard N (Dick) Anderson attended Penn State University and Columbia. He was a copywriter and executive for several ad agencies, including Benton and Bowles, SSC&B and McCann Erickson. He was a painter and professional jazz saxophonist. Dick died in Tokyo, Japan in 1974.

Lisa Anderson, who goes by Lise, studied anthropology and public health at the University of Michigan. She raised her family in Ann Arbor and worked at the university in health research for 25 years. She is a gardener, activist, and the author of *The Lost Chapters*, a memoir. She lives with her husband in Cornwall, Vermont.

www.ingramcontent.com/pod-product-compliance
Lightning Source LLC
Chambersburg PA
CBHW031050310726
48969CB00007B/2212